A REGENCY ROMCOM WITH A
Swan Problem

Get Thee Off My Lawn

DARIA VERNON

DAY BED BOOKS

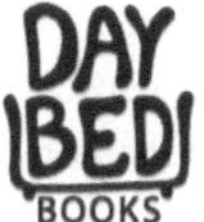

Get Thee Off My Lawn: A Regency RomCom with a Swan Problem

Copyright © 2022 by Daria Vernon

Print ISBN: 978-1-7359814-6-8

Digital ISBN: 978-1-7359814-9-9

www.dariavernon.com

Other Titles by Daria

HISTORICAL ROMANCE

~ The Rewards of Ruin ~

The Highwayman's Folly

The Rogue's Last Letter

DARK FAIRY TALE ROMANCES

Uncommonly Verdant: An Arborous & Amorous
Fairy Tale

The Sailor's Song: A Fairy Tale of Terror & Temptation

For Snowflake. Pretty bird.

(And for Zammy, Peggy, Mozey, Huey and all the other birds I've ever loved. Mean or not.)

1

Dorset 1808

April Nightingale would not stand for it. The swan was hers and the curmudgeon of Derring Hall could fight her for it. At eight-and-eighty years of age, he would lose.

Her gaze alit on the Derring pond as she crested the berm between their properties. Mr. Derring possessed three times the land of the Nightingale dower, but the pond itself was nothing to speak of. It was neither large enough nor clean enough to keep any swan properly content. And certainly not one so deserving as her Gerald.

She smiled when she spotted him—her little cygnet, all grown—looking proud and regal in spite of his overgrown surroundings. She'd have known him anywhere.

He'd had his fun, paddling about on the neighbor's pond for three days, but it was well into spring, and, at nearly three years old, he was due to pair with her other swan, Daphne, any day. The gentleman at the Dyers' hatchery had all but guaranteed a happy match.

April had kept an eye toward the garden for weeks, awaiting that moment when they would hook their necks in eternal companionship. She would not forfeit the goal merely because someone's lost hound had frightened Gerald onto Derring land.

She marched down the grassy slope of the berm. Any qualms over trespassing were quashed by the nobleness of her goal.

She called out as she approached the water's edge. "Gerald, darling!"

Hers was the first face he had seen upon hatching, and he usually perked at hearing his name, yet now he paid her no mind.

But April had not come onto Derring land unprepared. Armed with a fistful of crumbs, she removed a pinch and held it out over the water. "Gerald," she cooed. "I've something for you."

Gerald turned his back on her and kicked away.

She threw the crumbs onto the water, but they were ignored.

Worry shot through her. Had she waited too long to fetch him? Did he not remember her?

She hurried around the pond's edge to head him off on the other side. Here the bank was shadier. She swore under her breath as grasses, dried and overgrown snagged at her muslin hem. She was, however, pleasantly surprised to find Gerald continuing in her direction. She crouched into a teetering position at the water's edge. "There we are, love. Keep coming. We will get you home."

She sprinkled more crumbs in front of him. This time, he took notice, darting from crumb to crumb in front of her.

But there was a problem. While the other end of the pond had a gently sloped edge—the perfect beach upon which to lure a swan—here the soil dropped off steeply from erosion. How was she to lure him onto the grassy lip which rose two hands' height from the water?

She leaned forward, reaching for Gerald when he was near, but she could only just brush his wing with her fingertips.

She set down the rest of her crumbs and looked around for anything of use. The nearest tree had a thicket of sprigs at its base. She grabbed the woodiest one and gave it a tug. *Sturdy.*

With a firm grip on her anchor, she leaned out over the water. "Come Gerald. Be a good cob."

She could almost... nearly...

There!

With the sapling's support, she reached Gerald's back and tried to nudge him toward shore. He was, however, immoveable. How could a bird afloat be so rooted in place? "Come Gerald, you must hoist anchor for me."

She got down on her knees, grunting and sparing a thought for the stains she was inflicting on a dress that must last her the rest of the year. She stretched farther and secured an arm around Gerald's back. Her heart beat a drum of nervous triumph as she pulled him toward her, but he was suddenly less interested in staying put than in pulling away. And her, with him.

Her hand slipped on the sapling, bringing her nearer its end.

"Gerald!"

The snapping of threads at her shoulder seam was quickly outdone as the *snap* of most concern. Because the fragile roots of the sapling were snapping also. She released Gerald, scrambling to right herself before the sapling broke from the soil.

And just as the overstretched thing lost all tension in her hand, uprooting, she swung her upper half back onto the grass. She heaved a sigh that was both victorious and frustrated before hopping to her feet. She was greeted by the sight of Gerald with his beak turned up at her.

"Do not look at me like that! You *will* come with me. I do not care how ruined I am by the time we are—"

But that was all that came out—all she had time to say before being dropped into the pond, feet first, as the eroded lip of soil collapsed beneath her.

Her change in circumstance did not strike her straight away. Her first thoughts were not of how the water smelled nor how she was hip-deep in it. No, her first thought was that Gerald was nibbling crumbs right in front of her. Victory, in reach.

She wrapped both arms around him, wrestling him into an embrace she would have never dared otherwise. She grinned when his large feet tucked politely out of the way. She had what she came for. It was high time to leave. Only... she could not.

Her feet were swallowed by muck somewhere below the pond's filmy surface. The more she wriggled, the more she was suctioned down.

"*No,*" she breathed. She tugged one foot free only to lose her slipper.

Her distress spread fast to Gerald and his feet began to kick the air in front of them. She hugged him tighter, doing her best to keep his powerful wings pinned at his sides.

"Shh, Gerald," she cooed through her panic. "We will get you out."

"I do not think it is Gerald who needs getting out."

April's attention darted in each cardinal direction before she spotted the owner of the voice, a man, tracing the edge of the pond behind her.

She twisted at the waist and watched ruefully as a pair of polished black boots stopped, level with her eyes, above the fresh scar of earth.

Her eyes scanned upward, ever upward. Was he tall? Or was it a trick of her demoted stature? The stranger had a few years on her—just tipping, perhaps, into his third decade. Brown hair swished into a curl that fell over his forehead. All told, he cut a distressingly fine figure with the sun behind him, and the fact somehow added another heap of embarrassment to the already impossibly scandalous scene. April was no stranger to scandal, but this was hardly the sort she sought.

The man frowned, yet seemed to struggle to maintain the expression. A quiver in his cheeks betrayed oncoming mirth. "And just what is happening here, may I ask?"

April shrugged in answer. "'Tis a lark," she said.

"No," he corrected. "'Tis a swan."

He gestured to Gerald, who suddenly hissed and squirmed. April hefted the bird into a better grip and narrowed her eyes at her interviewer. "Does my predicament amuse you, sir?"

The man cocked an eyebrow and let forth some of his mirth in the form of a smug grin. "At the risk of being impolite... Yes. It does. Very, very much."

The smile he cast down at her was so light, so flippant... so *galling*. She could not help but notice how very dry he was, whilst she was very sopping. *Must be nice.*

"Provided you are not hurrying to some appointment, would you honor me with an explanation?"

"An explanation?!"

"As to why I find a fair stranger stealing a swan from Derring pond."

"Stealing? But you are in error, sir. The swan is mine."

"Yes. *Gerald.* I heard. Tell me, did any planning enter into this trespass?"

"The *plan* was that I could retrieve *my* swan and easily outrun the curmudgeonly master of Derring Hall given his advanced years... had it come to that."

"Supposing you could run at all," he gestured to her predicament, "then you are correct. You could outrun him."

"I am so glad we agree on something."

The man put his hands on his hips and looked to the sky. "I wonder though at a hole in your plan. Could not Mr. Derring's *son* catch up to you?"

"Mr. Derring has no children."

"Mmm. I see. That is strange."

"Why?"

"Because I thought myself, until just now, to be one of them. I must reevaluate some things now that a knowledgeable person has read me the facts."

Was the water suddenly colder? Surely it was. April squirmed, avoiding the gentleman's eyes, but she fared no better by staring at his breeches. Her cheeks flushed; was there no safe place to look in this position?

Gerald did not leave April much time to linger on her chagrin, freeing one powerful wing. The bird pummeled her face with it as he hissed and nipped her ear. She'd no choice but to let go and cower from the furious creature.

It was an eternity before he relented, taking flight to the most distant part of the pond.

Cowed, April turned back to the stranger. All there was left to do was seek mercy and hope the moment would never be outdone as the most humiliating of her life.

She had to wait for his breathless laughter to die down before she could speak. "How much did you see today?"

"Everything," said the man, through jovial gasps. "You must have called the swan Gerald at least a half dozen times."

April pressed her tongue to the gap in her front teeth and looked around, wary of any other potential witnesses.

"So... you are Derring's son then?"

"Leopold Derring. At your service."

"Are you truly at my service?" April gestured grandly to herself. "Because I will earnestly need it."

Mr. Derring folded his arms. "That depends. Who are you?"

April dipped a couple of inches into a scathing curtsy, wincing as the water reached higher. "Your father's easterly neighbor, Miss April Nightingale."

"Ah! One of the Nightingale girls." He bowed. "Miss Nightingale, a *most* unexpected pleasure."

"How is it you know our family?"

He shrugged. "The Nightingales have neighbored Derring land since I was born."

"But *I* have never seen you."

"Hmm. They should study that: How things do not exist if one Miss Nightingale has not seen them. Science is fascinating, is it not?"

The man's glee grew tiresome. "I agree, Mr. Derring. Science is fascinating. Particularly biology. Did you know, for instance, that this corner of Dorset is home to a very unique species of ass?"

Mr. Derring drew his lips between his teeth, grinning silently at her retort. She was so flustered by the fact he did not seem offended that she returned to staring at the inseam of his breeches.

"I agree," he said at last. "Biology *is* fascinating."

Her eyes snapped back to his as heat coursed up the sides of her neck. There was no more teasing in his dark eyes though. His lips rested in a gentle, serious line.

"I was away a long time," he said. "Both for my schooling and my career. A much older sister married young. Perhaps that explains our mystery."

April nodded and let his explanation end there. His brevity did not seem an invitation to pry.

The cold of the water suddenly racked her with a shiver. "Mr. Derring, might I ask—"

"Ah, right, your need of rescuing."

April was taken aback when he immediately shirked his coat and handed it to one of the tree branches for safekeeping. But then he stopped, putting a hand thoughtfully to his chin. There was the hint of a smile and it was clear that the more galling Mr. Derring was back.

"There is a problem."

"Oh?" April crossed her arms.

"I hesitate to rescue you when you are stealing my father's swans."

"He is *my* swan." April slapped the water with both hands.

Gerald kept his distance, maintaining a wary eye on them both.

"Swan!" called Mr. Derring. "To whom do you answer?"

Gerald honked.

"There, you see. It is a Derring swan."

April thought of calling Gerald's name, but the past fifteen minutes had been a lesson in where that would get her. She was in need of a more novel argument.

"If the swan is yours, Mr. Derring... then it must be marked." April grinned, pleased with her new tactic. "I think it best if I recapture it, so that we might check its mark and be sure."

Mr. Derring shifted on his feet. "I will grant you that it is an unmarked swan, thereby belonging to the crown. But my father is delighted that it has chosen our pond and he would not see it taken. Besides, is it not a greater crime to steal a king's swan than a neighbor's?"

Damn. April was out of arguments. It was time to subject herself to pleading.

"Sir." April swiped a damp tendril of hair from her eye. "Swan aside. Would you please assist me. I am quite mired in your filthy pond."

"Well, since you, sort of, asked nicely..." Mr. Derring took an urgent step forward, then retreated.

"There is another problem."

"Which is?"

"Your reputation. You see, if I extract you from the pond, I will be an unwed gentleman with an..." He paused, gesturing to her with an open hand.

April thought how best to answer, before uneasily admitting, "unwed."

"An unwed woman," continued Mr. Derring. "Wrapped in my strong, rescuing arms, wet petticoats clinging high on gamine legs—think how it would look to someone."

Gamine legs? Did she have such legs?

"You do not know what my legs are like," she said.

"True. The water is not clear enough and thank heaven for that, because your skirts are all afloat."

April looked down, horrified to see that white muslin bloomed around her like a lotus. She shoved the fabric down, disgusted less by the immodesty than by her nakedness in such rank waters.

Mr. Derring pointed toward his manor. "My housekeeper can oversee this for propriety's sake. She should return from her errand in an hour or so."

"An hour?!" Reputation be damned. "No. You cannot leave me like this."

Mr. Derring smiled. "I was not being serious. I will help you." He bent toward her with his hands on his knees. "But how can I resist teasing my swan thief?"

"I have noticed this about you—this 'not being serious.'"

Mr. Derring lowered his voice to a whisper that she could barely hear over the chatty springtime birds.

"If one were to come upon us, Miss Nightingale, I do not think they would find *me* the less serious."

Mr. Derring had loosened his neckcloth and it dangled within reach. She could grab it. Could pull him in. Could make him suffer for all his goading. But she did not.

Instead, she offered an admission. "I find that life needn't be so serious as everyone wishes to make it."

"Well said, Miss Nightingale." Mr. Derring tilted his head in an endearing way—a way that made the curl on his forehead flop to one side. He put his hands on his knees and stood. "Let's get you out of here."

He began to roll his sleeves. April's breath quickened—not with the anticipation of being on dry land but with something else... something familiar...yet suddenly more taboo than it had ever been.

Mr. Derring went to the nearest tree and wrapped his hands around a low, half-dead branch. He levered it, pumping it up and down while his bared forearms tensed and strained. It was not a lewd act, yet April felt strangely guilty in not looking away. She startled when the branch snapped.

He returned to the water's edge with a triumphant smile—lopsided, only one cheek pierced by a dimple. April could not help but smile back.

She was so mesmerized that she failed to shut her eyes when the branch's leafy end slapped the water in front of her.

She took a final, withering glimpse at Gerald—who spared not a glance for her—before wrapping her hands around the branch.

"Do you have it?"

"I think so."

Mr. Derring pulled her in, and she felt herself lose another slipper as she slurped free of the mud. She sighed. Her shoes would not be seen again—as lost here as at the bottom of the deepest sea.

She was only two steps nearer the bank when Mr. Derring abandoned the branch. He knelt and extended his arms to her instead.

She hesitated, struck by a premonition that the pond incident would be the least eventful part of her day.

Mr. Derring gave her a nod of reassurance as she took his arms and he took hers. His brown eyes sparkled with encouragement, and the firm warmth of his forearms sent a shot of confidence through her. "I've got you," he said.

With one solid pull, he had her to the edge. Then he wrapped an arm around her back and pulled her until her knee was on the grass—her *bare* knee. She had only just registered the fact, when she was pulled all the way upright.

A breeze whisked between her knees, confirming what she already knew. She was an unwed woman, wrapped in the strong, rescuing arms of an unwed man, wet petticoats clinging high on her gamine—

Mr. Derring kept her near as he reached down between them, tugging her skirts down from where they clung, preserving only the most useless bit of her modesty before he stepped away.

She shivered at the loss of his warmth and appealing dryness.

They stood in silence a few steps apart.

Then April asked the only thing that came to mind. "What now?"

2

Leopold Derring was at a loss over the view. Miss Nightingale looked like a river otter in a dress. Two strawberry blonde curls clung to the side of her face, damp and stretched. And her stockings, caked in scum, left him with the hard-fought urge to pinch his nose.

Yet he wanted to repeat the part where she had been in his arms.

She'd asked, *What now?* As though there were formal protocol on how to handle a drenched trespasser. A swan thief. A fetching filcher of fowl.

Anyone else he'd have sent marching swanlessly back to their own property, shoes or no. But this was no ordinary thief. This was Miss Nightingale. And her legs *were* gamine.

He did his best to hold his eyes on her drier parts

above the waist, but the damp muslin clinging sheerly to her thighs had infected his better judgment. He'd only seen it for a moment as he'd pulled her out, but the sight lingered like a glimpse of the sun after shutting one's eyes.

She was awaiting his answer.

"No one knows you came here?" he asked.

Miss Nightingale shook her head.

"Good. We must get you cleaned up." He took her hand in his, causing her eyes to flare. But the shock faded. Perhaps she realized, as he did, that "held hands" would be the least notorious thing about them should they be seen.

He was guiding her toward the house through the willow park when a shrill but gentle honk caught their attention. They turned.

A swan, neck stretched upward, waddled toward them.

"Gerald!" Miss Nightingale pulled away to greet it. "I *told* you he was mine." She knelt and threw her arms around the giant bird.

Leo glanced beyond their little reunion toward the pond, where April's originally alleged swan still floated. He pointed until she looked.

"Well," she amended, standing up, "I do have *a* swan on your property, but it seems I must apologize in regards to which one. Forgive me?"

She tipped her chin up proudly as she spoke, even as the stench of pond water wafted from her.

"Apology accepted. Besides," his eyes flicked briefly to her lower half, "you've paid price enough."

So. There truly was *a Gerald.* The swan followed them halfway up the park before distraction overtook him and he wandered off. Miss Nightingale looked worriedly after him.

Leo took her hand again. "He won't go far. I will see him returned to his rightful pond."

They continued to stalk through the trees, ducking from one to the next like little thieves. The nearer they got to the house, the more they played into the clandestine feel of it, pulling their backs against the tree trunks, darting glances this way and that, tripping over themselves in snorts of laughter...

Leo would try to hush her, then she him, but each half-hearted admonishment would only start the cycle of laughter anew. It had been so natural he could not recall how it had begun.

But now was the time to be serious. He pulled her under the last willow before the house.

"Why are we stopping?" she asked, breathless.

He cocked his head at the innocence of her question. Had it somehow not occurred to her how brazenly they approached his residence together? One of them soaked and disheveled?

He took a long moment to look at his swan thief.

A gap in her teeth was visible behind parted lips. A mole above her smile moved up and down in time with her panting as she caught her breath. She looked to be well into her second decade, a surprising age for an unwed woman, particularly one of such... well, *caliber* was not quite the word, was it? *Liveliness*, then.

"Here you must make a choice," he said. "We can enter one way and avoid all eyes, or we can enter another and bring my housekeeper into the situation."

Leo knew what he hoped she would say, but she did not answer straight away. He squeezed her hand, encouraging her to save him from his impatience.

She was still looking down in thought as she began to speak. "If you believe we can be discreet on our own, I wish it to remain as such. To keep it simple and secret."

Leo was already turning to pull her toward the house, when she squeezed his hand back. When he turned to her, they were nose-to-nose, secretive in the willow's protection.

"Will you be a gentleman?" she asked.

His loins nearly leapt to a response that would contradict him. He smiled. There was a certain tension in remaining gentlemanly that appealed to him very much. "You have my vow. But while I will do my utmost to keep us from view, there is the evergreen chance your reputation will be compromised."

"You presume much of my reputation."

"Oh?"

She tossed back her head in that confident way that he was beginning to find quite ravishing. "I will tell you this much, sir. Ladies found wrestling swans in others' ponds do not begin on the highest rung of marriageability. I have done worse."

"Enough said." But it was not, in fact, enough. Curiosity bloomed in Leo's mind. Where had she been before? What were her past adventures? And what future adventures did she threaten with that daring sparkle in her eyes?

He did his best to remain focused. "We cannot go by the front—our butler will be on duty. But we mustn't go by the servant's entrance either. There is, however, a terrace with an unlocked door. Are you ready for further adventures?"

"Do you not mean *mis*adventures? For that is all I have had."

He expected a pitiful look to follow—that same frustrated look of a half-drowned rodent from before. Instead, her blue eyes glittered—game and mischievous. The challenge he saw there took him aback.

"I suddenly wonder whether it is not *my* reputation that is more endangered by this connection."

"And wonder you ought. For it is you who will be forced to propose marriage should we be caught."

Leo scoffed, nervously hiding how little he was ruffled by the idea. "A consequence which flows both ways, Miss Nightingale."

Together they padded softly up the terrace steps toward a row of French doors.

"How is it we have only discussed *my* reputation?" whispered Miss Nightingale. "I know nothing of yours. Though, I suppose I approach that with optimism. I suspect no one a rogue until they reveal otherwise. So, are you a rogue, Mr. Derring?"

How fun it would be to call himself one, but this day brought the most excitement he had seen in a decade.

"No. I do not suppose I am."

"You sound unsure."

The chance to change his answer was there, waiting to be snatched, but while the day had turned playful, he could not lie about himself. Besides, they had reached the doors.

He pressed a finger over his lips. Silence was everything. He pulled down the door's handle and slipped stealthily inside. He shut the door behind her, softly as he could, but the sound still echoed in the cold, hardwood salon.

Leaning forward, he kept his boot heels from clacking on the parquet. Miss Nightingale's stockinged feet were of no concern in that realm. They still, however, proved troublesome; she was leaving a trail of puddles.

He pointed to her feet and her lips moved around a silent, *What?*, that made the mole above her lip dance in a spellbinding way.

He knelt and patted his shoulder, urging her to use him for balance as he took up one of her feet. Any woman he had ever proffered his arm for had placed her hand on him with feather light touch. Miss Nightingale had more of a griffin's grip.

He pushed her clinging skirt up over her knee and untied one soaking garter.

It was a pity making such short work of it. To not linger on the feel of his knuckles against her cool skin, or on how the fine hairs above her knee raised beneath his touch. His thoughts grew less gentlemanly by the second, making it all the more exhilarating to keep his actions pragmatic and cold. But could she appreciate a tease as much as he? It was a question he would stake the day on.

Her breath jumped as he pushed the clinging muslin up over her other knee with an open palm. Her reflex caused him one of his own. He had caught Miss Nightingale looking at his breeches in the pond; hopefully she would not resume the habit. He finished his work deftly, before his ardent organ decided to speak any louder.

With her garters and stockings slung in the crook of one elbow, Leo took up her hand once more. There was still a gentle *plip plop* of drips from her skirt as she followed behind him through the house. *Should have wrung her out in the grass. Too late now.* He doubled their pace.

They made it up the back stairs, making easy progress until—

Footsteps, straight ahead.

He jerked Miss Nightingale into the first open door, which they tucked themselves behind once inside.

He was so focused on the footsteps as they drew near and faded, that he'd not noticed which room they'd ducked into. As it happened, the first open door was also the *worst* open door.

It was the bedchamber once kept for his late aunt's visits and was designed to her vulgar tastes—rouge and gold—straight out of a Greek Street brothel.

Miss Nightingale was first to wander out from their hiding spot, when it was safe. She took in the gaudy view and turned to him with her mouth agape in what appeared to be mock scandalization. She delivered a hissing whisper, "*Mr. Derring,* you *are* a rogue."

He meant only to meet her with a stolen glance, but was held captive instead. Her smile, broad, yet secretive, was disrupted by the little gap in her front teeth. Paired with the previously noticed mole above her lip, the sight undid him.

He grimaced toward the luxurious bed. "Not very gentlemanly of me, is it?"

She brushed her fingertips along the brocade counterpane as she returned to him. "Is this room our destination?"

"It is not."

She placed her hand back in his, and he'd have sworn she mumbled, *"Pity,"* as they left.

They passed the top of the main stairs, holding their breaths as a maid crossed through the entry below. They passed his father's door too. He would be too absorbed in his atlases to notice two adults stalking through the halls like children.

At last they reached Leo's apartments and the door of his study was carefully clicked shut behind them. They leaned side by side against the closed door and let out grand sighs.

Miss Nightingale's panting morphed into a breathy laugh. "I feel as though we've snuck through a war encampment, rather than a sleepy country manor. That is, unless we are still in danger of your father?"

"Ah, yes. Was it 'curmudgeonly,' you called him? I would not worry. You were so very confident you could outpace him."

"Nearing his ninth decade, I should hope so."

Leo laughed. "My father is not yet in his seventh. And he is no curmudgeon either. Where *do* you get your information from?"

"My mother has never faulted me as a source before."

"Well, you may wish to reevaluate." He turned toward Miss Nightingale and noted her cheeks taking on a blush. Even in embarrassment, she never lost the confident tilt of her chin.

"I will find someone to bring up water for you." He gladly returned the fetid stockings to her care.

"Thank you, Mr. Derring."

For a fleeting moment, her face was so near that he could kiss her, but she stepped away from the door to let him out. He looked past his shoulder at her.

"I will be discreet."

Miss Nightingale shrugged. "I do not know whether you will or will not. I never finished determining whether you are a rogue. You were, after all, very stealthy at moving us through the house. Very sneaky. I wonder, do you have lovers you sneak off to see?"

"I do not."

"Do you have lovers which you *brazenly* see?"

"I do not."

"How then, Mr. Derring, do you see your lovers?"

Leo found no impudence in the question because he did not choose to look for it. He straightened and pulled back his shoulders. "As it happens, I do not have lovers at present, Miss Nightingale."

He turned to leave.

"But surely you have before."

The hairs on the back of his neck raised as though she had spoken the words right against him.

"Yes, Miss Nightingale. I have."

A smile was not what he expected to see when he glanced back at her, yet there was that charming gap in her front teeth.

"As have I," she said.

He fled then. Like a deer startled by a snapped twig.

His feet carried him swiftly down the hall. Had she just encouraged him? The "gentleman" in him was dying a fast death.

He was unused to Miss Nightingale's methods— to the ways her words found spaces between his ribs and pricked at something deep inside. Other women had beckoned him with coded turns of their fans, or slow, meaningful blinks. But Miss Nightingale had stood, dripping on his rug in bare feet, and stated plainly she was no virgin.

His urgency in departing shifted into to the urgency to return to her. He was wondering how the house could be so empty when Emily, the chambermaid, crossed through the entry below. "Emily!"

She startled, not knowing where to look.

"Up here. Hot water for a bath, please."

"Yes, Mr. Derring. Straight away." The young brunette vanished, making good on her promise of haste.

His heart pounded as he turned down the hall, no longer sneaking like a young boy but running like one, carelessly clipping the corners of tables with his hips.

"Partridge? Is that you?"

Leo halted, biting his lip. He'd made too much of a ruckus when passing his father's door. He opened it and let his eyes adjust to the curtained room. His father sat in a chair by the fire.

"Oh!" His father, Isambard Derring, tipped down his chin, regarding his son over spectacles. "I thought you were Partridge. Were you stampeding down the hall just now?"

"No."

"Hmm. Must have been all those caribou we keep." Mr. Derring rolled his eyes before pointing to something near his bed. "You are not Mr. Partridge, but you will do." He cast an impish grin at Leo. "Would you fetch that book by the bed?"

Leo went to the book, an atlas, of course. "Are you not well enough to take ten steps, Father?"

Mr. Derring perked up in mock defensiveness. "I will disturb my lap blankets! Besides, what good is old age if I cannot leverage it for a favor now and again?"

His father took the atlas from his hands and mouthed, *Thank you.* He'd been using his voice again for weeks—ever since the throat ailment that saw him in bed for all of January—yet was still in the habit of mouthing common phrases.

"Perhaps you are as good as Partridge after all. I suppose I will keep you around." Isambard's shoulders shook with a silent laugh as he waved off his son.

"Thank heaven I've a purpose in this life." Leo would usually linger and keep his father company. But right that minute, there was a Nightingale dripping on his floors. A rare bird, indeed. "Will there be anything else?"

His father smiled and shook his head, releasing Leo back to his escapades.

When Leo reached his study's door, there were already two footmen knocking at it, buckets of boiled water steaming at their feet.

3

April could not remember the last time she played at hiding. Age twelve, perhaps? Though, was it merely "playing at" hiding, when a very real consequence was knocking at the study doors? It felt the same, that rush in her chest as she heard the murmur of footmen in the halls.

She'd dashed to the only other door in the study when they announced themselves. And her heart had nearly stopped when she found herself no longer in a study but a bedchamber. It was as twice as large as any bedchamber in her own house, and had a broad, canopied bed, appointed in gray-blue silk. A touch more tasteful than the first bed they'd encountered.

And now she was under it, clutching at the mattress ropes and holding her breath. Hopefully, the footmen would not enter without their master's explicit welcome.

Her excited state had more to it than a game of hide-and-find though. She knew that. Her heart had not had a quiet moment since her spill into the pond. But her dunking could not compare to the thrill of being rescued by one Leopold Derring. To shut her eyes for just a moment—that was all it took to conjure the sight of his arms pumping the branch, or the feel of them around her back.

In youth, she had always attracted small adventures and affairs. It took little more than a wink or a flirty smile for it to find her—the absurdity that life offered in the shadows of formality. But the nearer she got to thirty, it seemed, the fun failed to show itself. No matter how much drama she sought to stir.

But her retrieval of Gerald was just the sort of farce her whims had once moved her toward. She basked in the familiarity of it. What had been forgotten, though, was that such amusements could be multiplied by a conspirator, and that such cooperation could result in days that were like gems in their joy and rarity. *Days like this.*

Here could well be the last gem for her. The rarest. She would seize it.

Another rush passed through her. One more sickening. The dread of an incomplete truth uttered to Mr. Derring.

Guilt fled, however, at the sound of talking in the hall. Her fingers tensed on the bed ropes as the study door creaked open. Then the bedchamber door. She held her breath.

Craning her neck to see out from under the foot of the bed, two boots took pause—the very same top boots she'd been level with in the pond. A heavy-looking bucket clunked down beside them.

"Miss Nightingale?"

She smiled and wiggled a hand up over head to snatch at Mr. Derring's ankle like a viper.

Her jape did not elicit the *yelp* she had hoped for, but there was a noticeable jump in his boot heels before an equally quick hand came down and caught her wrist. He got on his knees and peered under the bed at her.

"I wonder, would it ruin your reputation more to be found atop my bed," he asked, "or beneath it?"

"I'd wager both to be devastating but only one to make me less likely to be found."

He still held her wrist. "You know, I've a young cousin who is terrified of what lurks under her bed at night. Never again shall I belittle her concerns."

"Are you going to help me out from here?"

"Have I not helped you out from enough places today, Miss Nightingale?"

"Please." She wriggled until her other arm was

overhead and waggled all her fingers in a plea for assistance.

He grabbed her other wrist and pulled, sliding her out partway.

Mr. Derring came into view, upside down, where he knelt over her. The dark swish of hair over his forehead hung forward, joined by another wave or two. His dark eyes sparkled, even in shadow. She had no talent for the visual arts, yet wished she could paint the odd view and have it on her wall. Or her ceiling?

She was contemplating hiring an art tutor when he placed his hands on either side of her face. There was no thought then, just the instinctive preparation for something.

He stroked her cheeks with his thumbs. "You have brought a strange day to my door, Miss Nightingale."

Nothing was so strange now as hearing her surname on his lips. "April, will do fine now, I think. In honor of the strangeness."

"April, you may call me Leo."

She still did not know what was happening. Still waited on the cusp of something.

He pulled a cobweb from her hair and showed it to her.

"You are now not only damp, but covered in webs and dust. What will we do with your dress?"

"Remove it," she said, too quickly. "It must be rinsed and hung. It will take the *whole* day." She raised an eyebrow.

Her anticipation ended uneventfully as he pulled her the rest of the way out and helped her to her feet. He sauntered to a stand that held a quilted, dark green banyan and placed it across her waiting arms. "My dressing gown for you."

"You are quite generous to your trespassers, Leo."

He stepped near enough to her that she had to hug the heavy garment to herself. With hands behind his back, he leaned in until his lips nearly brushed her ear. "I do so wish to be neighborly."

April's shoulder shrugged instinctively as Leo's breath grazed the contours of her ear. She shut her eyes and let his words sink into her—an answer to hopes she could not deny.

She nearly staggered forward as he backed away; she had been leaning on his radiant heat as though it were a solid thing.

"Let me fix a bath for you before the water goes cold."

He lifted the steaming bucket and took it behind a tapestried screen near the window. The lip of a copper basin peeked out beyond the screen's edge and April positioned herself to see around it. Leo tipped the bucket against the basin's lip and an angry plume of steam enveloped him. The air in the bedchamber went thick with humidity and anticipation.

Leo looked back over his shoulder at her. The steam had made his dark lashes cling to one another and left water beading on his lips and cheekbones. He looked as though he'd toiled in bed over a lover for hours on a hot day. April hoped it a glimpse into her future.

He passed by her, fetching two more buckets from his study. She could not look away from his grip on the pails' handles—the way bulging veins wound up his forearms like vines. How would that grip feel on her thigh?

"You should get ready. The water will not stay hot for long."

April wiggled her fingers under the weight of the dressing gown in her arms, reminding herself of its existence, and hurried back into the study to change.

She fairly clawed at the bib of her dress to be off with it. She'd forfeit the whole of her meager dowry for the help of a ladies' maid for but two minutes.

At last she extricated herself from the wet, clinging muslin of her gown and petticoat. She looked down at her chest, heaving a sigh of relief that she wore wrapped stays more often than not as, at home, they could afford only one ladies' maid for three sisters and their mother.

The short stays were still *mostly* dry and she

hung them on a hook in the corner before peeling herself from a damp shift.

She draped the rest of her garments over a chair, nearer the window, and looked out over the Derring lawns, feeling like the ruler of them in her nakedness. She could see the Derring pond with two white, floating dots on it. She could also see the side of her home beyond the berm. She turned her back to the view, no longer pleasant.

She donned Leo's banyan, which could easily wrap her thrice, turning her into a little roulade if she wished. She bunched the spare fabric into her hands and enjoyed the feeling of its cool silk lining against her limbs. She dipped her nose to one shoulder and took a deep inhale. A spiced scent, like dark rum, clung to the fabric.

She faced the door. She had trespassed to seize a swan and would now seize something far better.

Leo was still behind the screen when she entered. She heard the gentle lapping of water before she peeked around its edge to find him kneeling, stirring one hand in the bath. Gentle steam still rose from it.

She cleared her throat and he looked up at her. Wordlessly, he extended a hand—an invitation that tugged her insides straight through the floor.

His eyes skimmed her up and down. His lip

quirked up. "You have nearly drowned twice today. Once in my pond and again in my dressing gown."

April stretched her neck long. "I keep my head above water, above cloth, at all times. That is not drowning." But she was drowning. Drowning in him. And his hand, still waiting for her to take it? It was about to pull her under.

His hand closed around hers and he shook the water from his other before pulling a stool to the basin's side. He guided her to sit, then looked up from where he now knelt at her feet. "How gentlemanly am I to be again?"

"Very," she breathed.

He drew the dressing gown aside until her knee was exposed. "Do I understand you correctly?"

"Your fluency is perfect."

Not merely perfect though. Leo was downright omniscient. He freed her other knee from the gown and somehow collected both her slender ankles in one hand.

April dropped a hand from her lap to keep the heavy gown from gaping any higher as she was swiveled on her seat—her legs, guided over the basin's edge by Leo as he stood.

She sucked air between the gap in her teeth as her heals kissed the steaming water.

"Tolerable?"

She nodded and he lowered her feet the rest of the way. Her breath hitched as he reached across the tub for a bar of olive soap on a silver stand. He pushed his rolled sleeves higher and lathered both hands, before relinquishing the soap back to the tray and dropping to one knee. Leaning over the copper lip of the basin, he glided his hands down her calf. He was deft but not delicate, cleansing her not only of pond water but months of stress as he squeezed her leg in long strokes.

The scent of warm, soapy water filled the air and there were no sounds apart from the lapping water and gentle *splishes* whenever Leo's hands dipped back in.

Bless you Gerald. Bless you for flying off. 'Tis a gift, this.

April released her grip on the overlarge dressing gown and one side slipped from her shoulder. The air against her breast was a kiss of refreshment in a room filled with steam.

Breathless, she watched the back of Leo's wavy crown of hair as he bent over the basin's edge. The back of his neck, slightly tanned, rose and fell as he worked. She reached for his nape, resting a hand against the place where trimmed hair tapered toward the top of his spine.

His skin turned to gooseflesh under her hand. His work slowed, but he neither stopped nor looked up. He was so serious. So deliberate. So unwilling to meet her gaze. Her impatience reached its acme.

"You are very good at cleaning your swan thieves," she said, combing her fingers against his hair, up to the crown where it was longer.

"You think I have cleaned the feet of more than one?"

"I do not know. I know very little of you, remember?"

"It is the frequency of swan thieves themselves which you overestimate." He finally turned his head, his dark eyes going beautifully wide at the sight of her breast. "You are too rare a bird to ever be seen before or since."

His words were a shot fired into the room. He held her eyes, seemingly awaiting a reaction. But April would never let him know how consciously she had resumed her breath once his words had stolen it.

His gaze did not release her, not even when he turned his head, just a little, and pressed his lips to the outside of her knee. He pulled back from the gentle kiss, but—with her hand still on his nape—she encouraged him to sear her skin with another.

He did.

She remained still as he abruptly stood. He moved behind her and she felt the heat of him at her back before he placed his hands on her shoulders. He lowered his face beside hers and spoke into her ear in a hot, sure whisper.

"April Nightingale. I am going to bathe you now. From your head to your toes. I will spare not one spot in between. *Not. One. Spot.* That would be the most gentlemanly, most neighborly act would it not?"

His fist had curled around the collar of the banyan, on the side from which it had yet to slouch. She knew he meant to pull it down. She turned her gaze on him, brushing his nose with hers, and met his eyes with intent. Then she shirked the banyan herself. "The most," she agreed.

Everything became a blur as she was scooped up roughly into hard arms. As she was carried to the basin's other side. As her feet and bottom met the water together. As she was settled against the basin's end. As she was hypnotized by the devilish depth of Leo's single dimple as he freed himself from his shirt-sleeves.

She coronated him in that moment with the crown of her trust, and she was his. However he wished her.

4

F or some, it was the eyes that betrayed the soul. With her? Leo believed it to be the little gap between her teeth. That was the keyhole she flashed at each mischievous turn and he was sure it led to worlds he could not fathom.

Somewhere beyond it lay the answer to her mysteries. To why a woman so odd and beautiful would go fast from his pond to his bedchamber. He was a student of her now, doomed to research her to his satisfaction. To become an expert, lest he squander his life's purpose.

And here was his first lesson, writhing silkily under his hand.

Serendipity danced in the room with them, the answer to a dozen lonely years. He'd traveled the world to cure that emptiness, yet each outpost only left him emptier. Now everything was full. The room. The house. The world.

And his hands. He'd filled his hands with the feel of her. Gliding them over every plane and curve of her. But he'd suffered the dizzying effects of his patience and restraint for long enough. And April had pulled and pushed his hands toward pleading places more than once. There was ample anticipation in the room to set the very air on fire.

He would keep his promise. Leave no spot untouched.

The water had cooled to a temperature that matched their own and everything below water felt the same as above, only smoother, softer, easier...

Her breasts peaked just above the surface, lathered in olive soap. He tipped handfuls of water over them and traced rinsing circles around them with one hand. Then he blazed a path down her stomach, over her navel, toward the soft, auburn patch between her legs.

Her flesh parted like weightless petals, and he thumbed at the small bud which they revealed. In response, April chased him with her body, melting into the tub until her lips dipped below. A moan vibrated through the bathwater.

The bud hardened like a pearl under his thumb. He had to feel her. Had to know the last inches of her. He slipped his middle finger inside of her and she arched her back till her whole head was submerged.

Leo reached his other hand beneath her neck, pulling her back up. "You said you would not drown."

She gasped a small laugh, even as she blinked water from her eyes. "It is too late for me. Save yourself."

"Nonsense, you must concentrate."

"On what? On how you play my quim like a harp? I cannot concentrate on anything else. Least of all staying alive."

Indeed she pushed greedily against his palm each time his fingers curled inside her. She dipped back below the water to make her point. He lifted her head again and took her mouth with his. She tasted, unsurprisingly, like olive soap. He ran his tongue across hers, then remembered that lovely gap and probed it. She was not shy about exploring his mouth in turn. When he finally pulled away, he had to tear away from the nip of her teeth on his lower lip.

"It is settled then. I will drown with you." Leo released her—both upper and lower halves—and braced a hand on either side of the basin, before forcing one of his boots off with the toe of the other.

"What are you doing?"

The first boot clunked to the floor. "Joining you." The second boot required his hands and frustrated him so much he threw it once removed. He removed his stockings.

His swan thief looked uncharacteristically horrified as he put one foot in the bath.

"But your breeches!"

"There's no time."

With a cock so hard and purposeful, would his clothes not simply dissolve or something? Surely the logistics would work themselves out.

April burst into laughter at his ridiculous answer, and his chest—and loins—warmed at the pleasure of making her laugh.

He stepped into the tub and bent over her, bracing his hands on the basin's sides once more. "Unlike yourself, I have many dry clothes at my disposal."

Her wide eyes continued to flick between his face and his fall. "But this is not how it is done."

"How what is done?"

She narrowed her eyes at his teasing. "*It.*"

He knelt in the bath, enjoying the way her face scrunched when his breeches became soaked through. "I've not found you to be shy with your words before this. Why so modest now?"

Fire came into her eyes, clearly stung by the word *modest.* She scrambled uselessly against the slippery bottom of the basin, trying to sit up. "I do not beat around the bush for the sake of modesty but for need."

"Need of what, dear April?" He so enjoyed teasing her.

She did not get her hackles up again. Instead, her face settled into something more serene, then smug.

"You give yourself away."

Leo hadn't the faintest idea what she meant.

"You need something too. Oh yes, it is jolly fun to tease and hold out on me. That was all I thought it was, but I see now the need for certainty in your eyes. Part of you indulges in restraint, but I fear you will not make good on the threat of ravishment. You are afraid of something. You need something of me too, do you not?"

The sense of play was gone, her tone, peeling him apart in the rawest of ways. His throat knotted at answering her actual question, so he skipped it over. He lowered himself farther, until his hard cock brushed against her belly through the fabric of his fall. He dragged his cheek against hers and spoke right into her ear. "I have not made any threats of ravishment, April."

"If you do not threaten it. Then I will."

"I know."

His words disarmed her but not for long. She put a hand against his face and pulled him nearer, holding him captive as she spoke her intentions, full and clear.

"If you do not ravish me, Leopold Derring, I will ravish you."

"You might try."

He tore away from her grip and looked her right in her pretty blue eyes. Was there still playfulness there? *Yes.* Only now, it was corrupted by lust.

Her hand grabbed his cock through his breeches. He groaned and a smile of triumph crossed her face.

What happened immediately after would not prove easy to recount. It was an explosion: a ball of limbs fighting for supreme position in the tub; piercing slaps across wet skin; the clanging of heads and elbows against the copper basin's walls; a battle on the scale of Hastings compressed into less space than a horse's trough. It was a wonder they did not break anything—either of themselves, or their surroundings.

And when the battle was over? When the shrieks and laughter died down? Only one was triumphant.

April sat atop Leo, straddling his hips. Her smile gleamed even more brilliantly than when she'd first caught his swan. She clutched his wrists—one in each hand. He had let her.

She'd been right to warn him of wet clothes. It was a terribly unpleasant thing, being trapped in soaked linen. Particularly now that the crux of two lovely legs was pinning his member. He grinned and nodded toward his fall. "Take your prize."

She raised a brow distrustfully but released one of his hands. He kept it high in surrender. Satisfied with this, she reached for his fall and began to free him.

In another moment, she had his rod in hand. She was not inexperienced, his April, and as she raised herself a little from her seat and handled him to aim him at her sex, he realized she was right. There was fear in him. There was need in him. And he did not know what was the cause of either.

❧

April lowered herself onto Mr. Derring's riled cock, piercing a well of anticipation inside of her so great she thought she'd burst. Her every muscle slackened in a sigh as she was filled by him.

She had it—had *him*—at last. It was the fastest she had ever been to bed—or bath—with any man, yet Leo had tormented her, making the minutes drag like weeks. She did not have weeks.

Their impassioned tussle had concluded with more water on the floor than in the bath, but she'd achieved her aim. Leopold Derring, the heretofore unknown neighbor, was between her legs. Her power over him, evidenced not by the winning of her position—he had let her have that—but by the expression on his face. Eyelids at half-mast. His dimple, shallow and serene. He was quiet now. Lulled away from his beloved quips and barbs by the feel of her cunny.

She smiled. Such a lovely prize was hers. She squeezed his hips with her knees just to remind herself of his piercing hardness and to stoke his visible need.

He bucked against her. Perhaps he feared she would tease him as he had her. Perhaps she had read him wrong and his patience had not been about some hidden fear after all. There was certainly no fear now. No hesitation as he encouraged her to move on him.

Her hands slid up from his wrists to lock fingers with him, and he offered his arms like two strong poles to support her as she rode.

She took him in long strokes first, loving the feel of his flared tip as it teased her entrance. And equally, she loved the unison of their moans as she plunged back down. With her on top, she was filled to blissful limitation. He bumped against something deep in her, something nearly painful—yet she repeated the motion again and again, loving how the sensation left a hollow in her stomach, causing a desirable tightness all through her.

She lowered one of his hands, placing it,

unflinchingly, where she wished it to be—palming her mound as she continued to rock against him.

Leo Derring was as great a surprise as ever she had had. She squeezed his hand in hers and dropped her head back in bliss as his other hand applied circling pressures to her mound. The unease of guilt was rinsed away. He wanted this the same as she. He wanted a day—a special, dangerous day—and nothing more.

He pulled her down over him and, stealing his hand from hers, wrapped it over her back.

She brushed noses with him and quickly turned her head to the side, but Leo's cheek brushed hers, tickling her with the sandy scrape of hairs only a half day old. Her lips kissed the water beside his shoulder as his breath washed over her ear. Each hair on her body raised with alertness, and the hollow within her grew deeper.

She could hardly move from her new position and Leo took control, thrusting his hips upward as he hugged her tighter. He found the tail of her fallen hair with the hand on her back and twisted it in his fist.

She was trapped against him—had lost her hard-won control... or had she given it up?

His cock was tilted into her. It threatened to leave her with every shallow stroke, rubbing her narrowest part with his thickest.

He removed his hand from her mound and replaced it on her ass. Warm water sluiced between their sexes, creating a lapping sound with each dip into her he took. With both arms around her, he controlled their joining, not letting it be lost.

His breath came nearer to her ear, and she prepared for him to speak. Instead, his tongue traced her ear and filled its spaces with heated breath. She reflexively pulled away from the strange sensation, before deciding she enjoyed it. She nudged her ear against his lips until he returned to the enticing task.

He did not let her stray from pleasure again, pulling her hair more taut with a twist of his wrist.

"You have a most exquisite cun, Miss Nightingale. How I love to fill it."

April shuddered, a prisoner against his feathery breath and fiery words. She was incapable of response, incapable, even, of telling where he ended and she began.

Her breath quickened as his strokes picked up their pace, guided easily by the rush of moisture that his words milked from her.

She pressed her hips against him, angling herself to feel the rub of his base against her. She trapped her most sensitive spot against him as they moved together. But he wasn't done.

"Will you come for me, Nightingale? Beautiful

bird? I feel your need. I feel how taut you are... how you must unravel."

He pulled her head back, until her throat was bared to a series of ravenous nips and kisses that made her shudder. Then he made her look at him, right into his bottomless eyes. He teased her nose with his.

A trembling whimper escaped as he held a stroke long inside her, nudging her to obey his command to let go.

He kissed her cheek before replacing himself at that unholy spot beside her ear—that place where he held all control. "I want to feel your pleasure grab hold of me. Come now. You are safe, dear April. Lose yourself."

The hand on her ass cupped her lower and lower, until she could feel his fingertips graze against the place where he drove into her. His touch removed any veneer of a dream. This was visceral. Carnal. *Real.*

Leo's lips moved over hers just in time to drown her eruption. His tongue and cock moved into her from either end and her bud pinched against his body one final time. She was gone. Shivering and jerking against him. Drowning. Just as she had sworn not to do.

His lips on hers reminded her to breathe again. She was coaxed back to life, drinking his kiss as though it embodied the whole act they had just taken part in.

But him... he had not yet...

Even as she came to her senses, even as she thought it. He drew out of her and sat up.

She clamored to do the same, hardly recalling she'd been in a trough of water.

He took his cock in hand, hiding its angry veins in his grip. He lolled back against the tub's opposite end and watched April while stroking himself. She would not leave him like that.

She straddled him once more. This time, his eyes were not heavy-lidded but wide open as she cupped the soft weight that hung below his rigid cock. She moved her hand upward, exploring the exquisite instrument that had just undone her.

The olive soap on its tray caught her eye and she rubbed her hand over its lathered surface before returning to her work.

Leo looked her in the eye. "I will not last long."

She smiled. "I know."

Once his cock was soaped, she rubbed her still tender parts against it. Letting her flesh gently splay as she guided herself back and forth along his length. It was almost too sensitive to bear after her recent rapture, but she could devise worse tortures.

Leo's head tilted back. His mouth, the mouth

that whispered with so much power over her just moments before, slacked open in weakness.

It was true, he did not last long.

His seed spilled down the sides of his shaft and kissed her sex warmly, before dissipating in the surrounding water.

He came almost silently, with little else but a low, growling purr. But his body stiffened in blissful rigor.

April reached forward and pushed the dark swoosh of hair back from his forehead. He tilted his chin down to see her and smiled, still breathing heavily from his release.

"It seems you've a soft spot for your trespassers, Leo."

"What I've a soft spot for, are beautiful women, with gaps in their teeth, who do as they please. Whether that gets them into my pond or my bath... or both, I care not."

She stuck her tongue to the back of her teeth, feeling the familiar gap.

Leo noticed. He put a finger under her chin and drew her nearer. Gently, he pulled her lip down with his thumb, urging her to show him. He squinted and turned her side to side by the chin. "Hmm."

Warmth spread over April at his silly assessment and she smiled, giving him the glimpse of it he wanted. He brought his gaze close to her smile before flicking his eyes up to meet hers.

"What do you keep in there, April?"

"All my secrets and dreams."

"It would be impertinent to ask your secrets but what of your dreams?"

The previous warmth fled, the bathwater suddenly giving rise to gooseflesh.

She did not say her answer, only thought it. *This. This is the dream.*

5

April pinched her muslin dress, testing it for dryness. The sunny spot where she'd slung it over Mr. Derring's chair had worked to its purpose. Barring any close scrutiny, the gauzy garment was ready to be worn.

But the thought of putting it back on made April well up. She assured herself it was because she had neglected to rinse it first, yet... disgust did not seem the reason for her emotion.

She tipped her head to her shoulder to feel the cool brocade of Leo's banyan against her cheek one last time and to inhale its glorious spice.

For hours, she and Leo had held one another, naked, on his bed. They talked of their favorite writers and their least favorite painters—he threatened to throw her out a window for calling Gainsborough overrated, but they could agree that Henry Benbridge had never seen a real person before. They talked of the best tricks they'd pulled on their siblings as children. The best meals they'd ever had...

But more than anything else, they recounted each part of their day together as though the memories were years old rather than hours.

Outside the window, the shadows on the grass were long. Her mother would soon return home from a day of errands. Young Anna would be delivered home by her music tutor. And Agatha would unfold from her den to drag herself downstairs and deign to sup with them.

To be back by supper was critical. April would have no excuse to rival her mother's expectation that they all dine together. If only they had a large enough house that she might be lost in it... *Where was I, mother? Oh, just in the darkest nook of the eighth floor library of the southwest wing.*

April longed for the shadows outside to recede, to reverse their direction until the day was brought back to morning. She wished her day with Leo had come before this—months ago, years ago... It was the perfect reminder of the manner in which she loved to live. But in the time since, she had acquiesced to a commitment that was as offensive to her sensibilities as it was necessary to her household. Days such as these would be impossible.

What if they had met then? What if Mr. Derring had wished for something more?

April severed the thought as her eyes drifted back to the horizon outside. The Derring land was deep. The house, grand. She had no delusions as to their difference in status.

Mr. Derring had known nothing of her spotty reputation but had now experienced it firsthand. Had dabbled in it. Had left his dye in the darkened waters of her "purity."

The shadows outside refused to reverse themselves, so April hugged the large banyan more tightly around herself and wandered to a map on the wall. It depicted a large island, but the language of its labeling was unknown to her.

It was beautifully rendered. An illustration of a brigantine, in the lower sea, rode on swirling waves and parted billowing clouds. A sea monster jutted from the water near a beautifully decorative compass.

"Iceland."

April swirled around. She'd not heard Leo enter. He had clocked stockings and a pair of old-fashioned, red-heeled shoes in one hand—pilfered from his aunt's old wardrobe no doubt. He closed the door softly behind him and came to where April stood at the map.

"It is the most beautiful place I have ever been," he said.

"You have *been* there?"

"I drew the map."

April wanted to know so much more. How he came to be there, where he learned to render things so beautifully... yet all that came out was, "And there are sea monsters?!"

Leo laughed. "I was young when I did this one and had not yet seen a whale before. Let us say, I was mistaken in its attributes."

April looked back at the creature, regarding its batwing fluke with new eyes. She had never seen a whale in person either. They might look just as monstrous anyway.

"You drew this?"

"I loved cartography. It was a hobby of mine."

"A hobby you traveled very far for."

Leo shrugged. "A career, then."

"And what need of a career? I was under the impression your family has been landed for generations."

"Did your mother tell you that too?"

April's cheeks heated, but Leo smiled.

"That, at least, is true. But suffice to say I had an urge." He turned his dark eyes on her. "You understand urges, I think."

She did. And the urges she'd satisfied in his bath left a trail of more behind them.

"Is that where you have been for years? Is that why I had never seen you? You have been traveling and drawing the most beautiful maps?"

He smiled and she hoped it was because her compliment had struck him.

"That was the idea. But there is this damned thing that kept getting in the way: Promotions."

"I do not follow why promotions would be unwelcome."

"The men who commissioned my work knew me capable of what they saw as 'more.' Suddenly I was not quietly taking sketches and measurements home to my study, but was having dozens of men put under my leadership for grueling years-long surveys."

Leo sidestepped to put himself behind her. He wrapped an arm around her, just below her breasts and rested his chin on her shoulder. She leaned her head against his cheek in kind as they stared at the framed map.

Leo tapped on the map's key with his finger. "This one's measurements are far from accurate. My brushstrokes are poor, my lines uncertain, my Icelandic *appalling* and my whales..." He turned and rubbed his nose against her cheek. "Well, they are the thing of nightmares, are they not? This map is terrible in all the ways I would later improve, yet it reflects my love for maps the best."

"It is hard to hold onto the things we love in youth. No matter how strong we are, it seems life has a way of pulling us away."

"And what occupies your clever mind, April?"

"Apart from an obsession with swan husbandry?"

He laughed softly, tickling her neck. "Apart from that."

How did his lips always end up so near her ear? Did he know how intoxicating it was to *feel* his words wash over her?

She shrugged. "I garden."

An embarrassing silence followed her words, and she hastened to make a joke of it. "In Iceland. I garden across all of Europe and it is very interesting. I sail the seas and am truly a very interesting person."

"If there is anything this day has taught me, it is that you needn't worry over how interesting you are. I'd wager you are far more so than myself."

There was something about his earnest diffusion of her jest that haunted her. Something gentle in his eyes, something so full of truth it made her ill. It was a very different man than she had met that morning.

"I was once much more social," she offered, ceding herself to the safety she felt in his arms. "I may not have been on the seas, but I was out there. In the village. In the land. And now I am mostly home, only dreaming of the things I did before. I do not know what has happened to me."

"We grow different over time, April. The march of the clock makes us want different things."

"Today had me missing how I used to be."

"You needn't think of it as some dead part of you..." He kissed her neck. "It is merely in balance with all the other, newer, parts of you."

April stared deep into the chart of Iceland, trying not to lose herself in the feel of Leo's warm lips against her neck. She shivered suddenly, not at his touch, but at the discomfort of having shared something too intimate.

"I need to leave soon," she said.

Leo nodded and looked back to the map.

"Do you suppose anyone heard us?" she asked.

"My dear April, *everyone* heard us."

She gasped in dread. "Even your father?"

Leo's face pulled back as though there was a bad smell. "God, no, not him. His rooms are the other side of the stairs and he was either reading or napping. The staff, however, have an ear for these things."

April stared at him, astounded that his face did not reflect her anxiety.

"Worry not. They are discreet." Seeing her face did not change, he added, "I told you, I have had lovers before," and winked.

April walked to the tall window. The pond seemed so far. "Then why did we... why all of the sneaking about?"

Leo cocked his head at her, and she smiled before he even uttered his answer. "Because it was fun."

Her shoulders untensed. "It was, wasn't it? The most I've had in years. But you are too unbothered, I think."

"You see right through me. The house staff are smart, but not omniscient, there is still your identity to be preserved. We should sneak you back out."

"Will you draw me a map?" April pointed at his piece of art.

"April Nightingale, I will never draw a map to see you away from me..." He took two strides forward and kissed her, lingering over her lips once he pulled away. "I shall only draw maps to bring you back."

April's thoughts churned over his words as she dressed. And as he asked interested questions, her mind was elsewhere. The shadows of the trees outside continued to encroach at horrible speed.

It seemed no time had passed before she and Leo were on the berm between their lands, bathed in the golden light of late day. Her lips still tingled from goodbye kisses, and she had a swan in her arms. Gerald. The *real* Gerald.

Leo combed his fingers over her ear, through the

hair she had hastily redone, then looked her in the eye for what she knew would be one last quip:

"Now go, April Nightingale. Get thee off my lawn."

His dimple deepened one more time before he made a shooing motion.

Then Mr. Leopold Derring headed down the hill, waving back at her. He grew smaller and smaller, nearing the towering home she'd never once seen him come out of and worried she never would again.

It would be wrong to stop him, though. Wrong to call out. Because by the week's end, she would be married to a man picked out for her by a desperate mother. A man she had never met.

6

Three days had passed since Leopold had found a swan thief in his pond—the same pond he now stared down at in melancholy.

The surface was filmy and green as he stabbed a long-poled net into the shallow. Thus far, he'd dredged up little else but a pile of algal mud and one frog, to whom he apologized before tossing it back.

But finally, a pointed shape jutted from the net. One slipper, found. He held the mud-caked shape as far from him as possible as he freed it from the net and rinsed it.

More than once, the Derring swan—unmarked and wild—caught the corner of his eye. Each time it did, it tricked him into thinking—into *hoping*—it was Gerald. It never was.

Rinsing the shoe revealed patches of a soft,

stormy blue but did not restore the object to its former condition. Far from it. And another hour of effort did not reveal its mate.

After all his hard work, there was still no excuse to see her. All he had was a shoe. A symbol to obsess over like a prince in a French fairy tale.

He looked east toward the berm between their properties. How long had Miss Nightingale been cloistered in that house of rubble masonry?

It was, perhaps, fairer to ask himself how long he'd been away from Derring Hall. He'd traveled for so long, overseeing land surveys that took him further and further from his original passion. *Was it eight years now? Ten?*

Then he'd received a letter from his father. It requested nothing of him but was laced with those subtle reminders that time marched on: "creaking knees," "poor appetite," "late to rise." A pang in Leo's heart told him it was time to come home.

There were no regrets when he did. He had not recognized the depressing effect of his work until he was far removed from the highways he'd been "promoted" to planning. Yet a return to Derring Hall did not make him magically contented either.

On return, he found his father unwell. Isambard Derring had weathered the ailment well for his age, but the bedrest had left a strong man weak, and he was slow to be coaxed outside for air and exercise.

Derring Hall suddenly felt languid and empty and... so very large. Leo's father was the last joy that filled it up. Someday he would be gone, and how then would Leo fill such a place?

The manor had seemed quite full just three days earlier, when April's spirit had brought light to every corner. Each morning in the days since, Leo had ensured that every drape was opened, but he could not make it so bright again.

April had made the world young and lovely in a way that could not be replicated.

Leo pined for a glimpse of her on the berm. Longed for her to emerge from his pond like a water nymph. At the very least, he wished Gerald would show. At least that would grant an excuse to...

The thought planted a mad idea in him, and his gaze darted to the berm. *It would not be so mad, would it?* He dropped April's murky shoe on the grass and hopped to his restless feet. Three days was long enough.

Not a minute later, he was on the berm, breathing hard from his little jog and concealing himself behind a tree. He scanned the Nightingale property. The two-story house of rubble stonework was tidy and symmetrical and faced a pond much wider, and admittedly more well-kept than the Derring pond. He was disappointed, however, to note the water feature's nearness to the house. It was in full view of the front-facing windows. But there, in the shade beside it, was a swan. *No.* Not one swan, but two.

He felt bold as a soldier as his plan took shape—as he charted a path to the pond from tree to tree. The low shrubbery would be enough to conceal him if he crawled the final distance. After that, it was just a quick dive and a roll to reach the—

The door of the Nightingale house opened. A woman in a white round gown and bonnet waved others on to join her. Three young women followed in procession, the last being April.

Leo's breath caught. He tucked himself further behind the tree. Three long days he had pined for a glimpse of her, yet she was not the same. Her sandy hair still sparkled reddish in the sun, and her long arms still dangled somewhat awkwardly beside her, yet... if not for these things, he'd not have known her. There was no spark in her as she tied on her straw bonnet. Sedately, she hung a reticule on her wrist and shut the front door. Then she followed her two sisters with her eyes to the ground like a sad cygnet.

Leo's heart squeezed with worry. *Just a bad day,* he hoped. What day, after all, could live up to the one they so recently shared? Perhaps she was as tormented as he.

The good news was they were departing. Headed toward the village by the looks of it. Mrs.

Nightingale counted shillings in her palm before dropping them into her reticule.

Leo sighed. His grand plan—of darting and ducking and diving—dissolved. He could merely walk over the berm and kidnap poor Gerald. Should any servant spot him, he'd merely insist on the bird being his. If April could do it, so could he.

It was, indeed, that easy.

He looked up at the Nightingale house in disappointment as he stood before it. He ached to be "almost caught," to feel as young and ridiculous as he had with April. Seeing no one in the house's windows to challenge him, he turned his attention to the wide, glistening pond.

The swans still rested in the shade beside the drive. They were on dry land and he wished them to stay that way. While he hoped for adventure, he did not wish to be so over-blessed with it as April had been when she fell into his pond.

His plan, though, struck a hitch:

Which swan?

The two swans in the shade did not wear ribbons with their names on them and their elegant faces were distressingly uniform.

The pair picked at bugs in the grass with their bills while Leo thought on it. Then—an idea.

"Gerald!" he called.

The one farthest from him looked up. The

method was dubious, but offered as good an answer as he might get. If it yielded the wrong swan, so be it. April did not seem the sort who would give *any* swan leave to abandon her.

Leo checked over his shoulder at the house again. Its stone facade, clutched by sheets of ivy, stared down non-judgmentally. It was going to let him get away with it.

The swan that hadn't responded to his call waddled warily into the water as Leo approached. But the other—Gerald, presumably—stretched his neck tall and looked at the pond, seemingly with the intent to follow his friend into it.

It was as fine a time as any for Leo to get the exercise he desired, so he dove for it. For Gerald. And Gerald hardly moved, allowing his assailant to nose-dive in the damp soil beside him. He took a nonchalant nibble of Leo's hair before Leo scrambled forward to gather him up.

Leo stood then, rather pleased with himself and rather surprised to find how heavy swans are. Thankfully, Gerald proved as tame with Leo as he'd been with April.

Leo crossed back over the berm with a bounce in his step and a swan in his arms. Gerald's feet and neck stretched out in front of the pair as he observed the passing landscape. Yet as the Derring pond came into view, Gerald's legs began to kick.

"Oh, you see the water, do you? I bet you would like to be in your favorite pond today, would you not?"

But Gerald was not placated by Leo's reassurance. He began to kick enough that Leo set him down long before they reached the water. The feisty cob stretched his neck and wings, doubling in size in all directions and ran eagerly toward the pond.

Leo had not thought much on the size of swans before, but he acknowledged that the bird could probably best him in a fight. Suddenly April seemed a warrior in how she'd handled a wild swan in the pond. How ever had she captured such a beast?

Gerald hopped into a fierce and short flight before splashing down in his favorite place. He folded his wings and twisted his neck in an impossible way before tucking his bill into his downy back.

The wild swan of Derring was on the pond too, seemingly unbothered by the visitor.

Leo smiled, pleased by his hostage's contentment. How easily things had fallen into place. He glanced in the direction of the village.

Now it was time for the ransom.

7

Anna held a lavender ribbon to April's throat. *Just strangle me with it already*, thought April. But sweet, oblivious Anna would notice none of the annoyance in her eldest sister's eyes.

"You are right, Mama, perhaps the yellow *is* better." Anna armed herself with the yellow ribbon and thrust it in place so quickly that it *did* briefly strangle April.

Beyond Anna's shoulder, Mama's face showed concern. "'Tis more apt for a wedding," she drawled. "I said it would be."

"What do you think, Agatha?"

Agatha, the middle sister, leaned against a counter by the shop window, playing absently with her bonnet's ribbon. She shrugged. "I do not *care* what color she wears to wed Mr. Gramble, only that it is done."

"Agatha!"

Alas, Agatha had heard her mother say her name in the same astonished tone a thousand times before; it put not a dent in her stubbornly dreary constitution. As second oldest, she was the one most looking forward to her spinster sister's exit. She saw it as the clearing of her own path toward marriage. Apparently, it was the singular thing that, at twenty-five, left her unclaimed. Never mind that her sour attitude was constant or that she forced off-key songs on each potential suitor. No. *Surely* it was all April's fault.

Regrettably for April, the family matriarch had bought into the idea. Which was why April was to be shuffled off on the arm of one Mr. Gramble. For the good of Agatha—half as amiable but twice as chaste, and therefore, a catch.

Anna was only nineteen and was both amiable *and* chaste. Though April saw in her youngest sister a spark that left her open to corruptibility. She longed to encourage such corruption but knew where that had gotten her. She had no desire to see Anna hurt the same.

In fact, it had never hurt so much. Not before this week. Not before her taste of a mysterious neighbor who appeared out of the ether and disappeared just the same.

"Perhaps we can do lavender for the tea then?" suggested Anna.

Sweet Anna cared very little whether her sister was married or not, and cared very much about how she would look doing it.

"That will do," their mother agreed, not taking her eye from a straw-colored parasol for sale. Today her mother would put the parasol back without purchasing it, but she would likely return for it once the papers were signed, once their family was under Mr. Gramble's financial protection. Once their pockets were filled with the rescuing wealth of his ill-gotten imports.

The Nightingales were not destitute, but nor did they live as they had when Papa, the personal physician to the Duke of Montrose, was still alive. For fifteen years hence, their circumstance had slipped, and Mama was unaccustomed to such a slight allowance, one granted to them by an inheriting cousin with whom they had thin ties.

In her mother's eyes, Mr. Gramble was a dream match for April. A miracle suitor who had to be snatched before whispers of April's improprieties reached his prominent ears—at least, his ears *seemed* prominent by way of the portrait he had sent ahead of him.

He was older, brushing against fifty years. The

portrait did not make him look so terrible, but April struggled to imagine much in common with the man.

Anna and Mama warbled on about a third type of ribbon and April took the chance to slip away, running her fingers along the counter that Agatha was sulking against.

"Are you choosing any new baubles for yourself today, Agatha?"

Agatha grinned. "I will wait for my own wedding day to choose such things."

"Oh? And who will you wear the ribbons for? Nothing short of a king, I suppose."

"I shall wear them for whomever I love, because *you* will no longer be sinking the household into a bog of ill repute." Agatha flicked a finger against April's sleeve for good measure.

"I have never been caught at anything."

Agatha rolled her eyes. "And yet we all *know*. Strange, that."

"Do you think my lot cannot be repeated with you?"

"You mean, am I going to stain my own reputation with sordid affairs?"

"I have seen you flirt. You are not immune."

Agatha snorted. "Flirting is a far cry from lying with a man."

April smiled and pretended to think before

leaning close to her sister's ear. "Sometimes it is less of a far cry and more like a few minutes."

"You are disgusting. I would never."

April grinned again. When her sister resorted to such derisive language, it meant April had won.

Agatha took a fuming breath and reared back for another strike of her tongue, but a knock at the store's window cut her off.

April's eyes snapped up, and she could not believe what was framed by the windowpane. There was Leopold Derring, smiling at her.

Her face burned with how fiercely she smiled back.

But Leo gestured toward the door of the haberdasher's shop. He meant to come inside.

As he disappeared from the window April's smile turned down. *This cannot be happening.* By the time he entered the shop, she was in full panic.

There was no place to hide, so she waved him, reluctantly, to their little circle.

"Mr. Derring," she cooed. "What brings you to the village?"

He opened his mouth to speak, but paused, seemingly unprepared to answer before a whole watch of Nightingales. "I had business here. Things... needing tending to. Business things."

Mama cleared her throat in a way that, in her

youth, might have been a delicate suggestion but was now a full hack.

"Mr. Derring, my mother, Mrs. Charlotte Nightingale. Mother, this is our neighbor, Mr. Leopold Derring. Have you not met before?"

Mama eyed him suspiciously even as she dipped her head.

"Mr. Derring, the younger," he appended, doffing his hat.

"I have only met your father, Mr. Isambard Derring, long ago. We did not part on amiable terms."

Anna gasped at their mother's forwardness, and April was left in similar shock.

Leo, for his part, took it in stride. "I am very sorry to hear that, Mrs. Nightingale. It is a good thing for us then, that this disagreement was long ago."

She pursed her lips. "Mmm." It was neither an agreement nor an expression of further disdain.

Anna fairly bounced in her slippers for an introduction. It struck April then that she was not the only Nightingale who found Leo handsome. Even Agatha was leering.

"Mr. Derring, my younger sisters, Miss Agatha Nightingale and Miss Anna Nightingale."

"A pleasure," he assured them.

Anna glowed in his presence while Agatha went blank, looking like she was caught up in a water wheel. At last, she shook it off, remembering to be nosy and suspicious, as was her wont.

"And how do you know our sister, Mr. Derring?"

April dreaded any hesitation in his response and was ready to leap on it herself, but he was prepared.

"An unfamiliar swan landed in the Derring pond this week. It turns out it was Miss Nightingale's, so I—"

"*Ugh*. Gerald." Agatha rolled her eyes and crossed her arms.

"Ah," said Leo. "It seems his *fowl* reputation precedes him." Leo paused for laughter but only a quick, shrill laugh from April filled the gap, leaving everyone else shifting in discomfort. He straightened and continued. "Miss Nightingale came over the berm looking for him, and I came to her aid to see him home."

Leo met her eyes with a fleeting glance that made her knees buckle. Would he dare elaborate?

"With the help of my housekeeper," he lied, "we all saw Gerald back to Nightingale lawns."

Kind of him to make mention of a chaperone, thought April, as though any level of scandal could harm her now... or save her.

April's whole family looked to her expectantly and she shivered with a frisson of annoyance. "Such a headache, that Gerald."

It was a good thing she was no actress, for her delivery was deserving of rotten vegetables.

Leo laughed, but not cruelly. She was warmed by how he saw through her. "Best prepare a cool cloth for your next headache then. Because he is, I regret to say, back on my lawns as of this morning."

"No," she gasped, annoyed by the sincerity of her disbelief.

Then she realized what it meant. A reason to see more of Leo. To walk with him. To be with him. An excuse to push her mother and sisters and future to the periphery for just a moment longer. It was, she realized, *all* she had wanted for days.

"I am afraid 'tis true. He has a penchant, it seems, for the Derring pond. I expect you will be 'round to retrieve him?"

"Oh, leave it," said Mama. "He is a mean old bird." Her eyes shot to Leo. "May he live a long life on your pond."

Leo smirked. "Why thank you, Mrs. Nightingale. My father will be pleased to learn we have the gift of new waterfowl from our neighbors."

Mama's eyes predictably widened. "On second thought, the beast is our responsibility. We would not want him biting anyone."

"Biting?" asked Leo. "I admit, I did not see it in him. He was nothing but sweet when we met this morn."

It was April who interjected with her scoff. "Impossible. He is only docile with me."

"'Tis true," said Anna. "I have a scar on my hand from him. See here." She tore off a glove and thrust her hand at Leo, who politely entertained the showing-off of her scar. The male attention sparked a bashful giggle in her.

April turned to her mother. "I shall go over the berm to see Gerald home once we are back." April turned to Anna, knowing she would never get away with it without company. "Would you like to join me?"

But before Anna could give her all-but-certain answer, Mama held up a hand.

"You will not have the time, April. You must write the menu for tomorrow's tea."

"A tea?" asked Leopold, anything but innocently.

"You must come!" spat Anna.

Mama put a finger to each of her silvered temples and applied a swirling pressure. "If Gerald is April's headache, these girls are mine."

Leo did not answer her mother's offhand comment. But before Mama could unlay the path of invitation, April cut in. The conversation *had* to end without further mention of the tea. The *engagement* tea.

"Then perhaps Mr. Derring would be so kind as to see Gerald back over the berm once we are home."

April saw the faint collapse of hope in his eyes. She could do nothing to bring it back, no matter how hard she wished. Moments before, she had been ready to throw herself back over the berm, but at the tea's mention...

She could not. *They* could not. And she could not even tell him why. Her heart felt leaden.

She would write him later. She would confess and thank him for the blessed gift of their affair.

"Of course," said Leo. "I will be happy to see him back.

"It will be nice having both swans in the pond again," said Anna, all heads swiveling toward her. "They will look so romantic for the nuptials on Saturday."

And there it was. The words that emptied the air from the room, the thoughts from April's mind and the color from Mr. Derring's fine face.

April's feet sank into the shop's plank floor as though it were the muck of the pond all over. *Trapped.*

She dared to look at Leo and was horrified to see he was still innocently happy.

"Nuptials, you say? Who here am I to congratulate?"

His eye met April's and suddenly he knew, and she knew that he knew, for his soul floated away from his body like an ember.

"Me."

It was a whimper, gentle as she could manage as she tried to keep him from shattering into any more pieces.

She had told herself to that point that she had done no harm, that it would be as impossible to hurt him as it had the other rakes she'd lain with, many who had, in fact, hurt *her*.

He had all the makings of a rake: the wit, the charm, the beauty... So she had filed him on the same shelf as the rest of them.

But her dread in that moment revealed it to be a lie she'd told herself.

After all, he'd wished only to draw maps that saw her back to him. Did it mean he'd longed for something more? More liaisons? More...

She resisted completing the thought.

But she could see in his eyes what it did to him to know. His gaze was lost and strained all at once.

April's fists balled at her sides. *The same as any affair,* she told herself. *The same.*

She forced herself to smile, and he braved one also, one so believable that only she could see how hollow it was.

"That is very happy news," he said.

If only it were.

Leo dipped his head at his bevy of new acquaintances and studiously avoided April's eye as he donned his hat.

"Mrs. Nightingale. Ladies."

His gaze paused on her, and his eyes silently added her name to his curt list of departures. *April.*

His brave smile tightened. "I will, later today, return your swan. Enjoy the rest of your errands."

He had such a wind behind him as he left that his coattail was nearly caught up in the shop door. He was gone.

"There goes a fine-looking man," said Agatha.

"Do not even think it. He has bad blood," Mama insisted, rather curtly.

April's attention turned to her. "How, Mama? What is your grudge with Mr. Derring?"

Mrs. Nightingale adjusted her posture. She often did so when trying to add an air of dignity to something petty. "I tried to befriend him some years ago and found him repulsively impolite."

April stared at her mother, expecting more but nothing came.

"I should fetch Gerald later today," said April.

"You should write a menu," said Mama. "And you should wear the yellow on your wedding day."

8

"Gerald, you frivolous twit! Get your feathered ass here at once!"

The bird Leo had found so tame and amiable upon its kidnapping had turned coats on him, donning an attitude more common to swans: that of a goblin.

Leo had—wisely, in hindsight—removed his polished boots and left them behind on the grass before getting more than the toe of them wet. Thus far, he'd prided himself on this not going the way of Miss Nightingale's mishap.

Yet his hubris ultimately saw him up to the thigh in the same brackish water. He blamed it on his mood. He'd removed his boots and coat and rolled his sleeves as though preparing for a brawl and perhaps the bird had sensed it on him—that need to express a dark feeling by way of a little sport.

Gerald was the one gloating though, preening his feathers and kicking around at the far end with the resident wild swan. Leo looked at them together and wondered for the first time whether the wild swan was a cob or a pen. Perhaps they liked one another's company.

Leo's shoulders fell at the thought. Because he, too, liked someone's company and that someone had carved a deep wound in him. He resented it all the more for being unintentional. After all, he had never attached such expectations to a tryst before, why should she?

Further, what *were* his expectations? He could not identify anything tangible, only knew he was made unwell by it—that he had not been right for the rest of the afternoon. He had the most dreaded sense that he would not be right again for many months or more.

In his quest for distraction, he'd pursued a beast of a bird for the better part of two hours, when a bit of patience might have served him better. He'd weathered nips and pecks from both swans, as well as a powerful beating from wings as wide as he was tall. His forearm was bleeding and scratched. He was as defeated by the swans as he was by his own heart.

As the dreadful ache in his chest began to swell

again, he swatted his hand against the water, splashing the bird who toyed with him just out of reach.

This was a mistake.

Gerald's neck uncoiled from distracted preening and turned a bead-like eye on Leo. Leo could *feel* the wickedness in that look.

He squared off with the creature, adopting a wide, defensive stance. Yet the gleam of seriousness in the beast's eye warned him to deescalate. "Gerald, fellow, I thought we were friends."

"*Sssssssssss!*"

Leo did not like that sound in the least.

"We must get you back home now. Your mistress will be anxious to see you. Do you not wish to see April?"

Gerald turned, gliding menacingly toward him, beak upturned.

Pulling a foot from the pond's sticky bottom, Leo began a backwards retreat.

"Come now, you *love* April. She is kind to you, is she not?"

"*Screee-pshht*"

Leo was unsure whether the shrill sound was a happier noise, but chose to take it conversationally.

"Yes. She is. I agree. Very lovely..."

"*Pshht*"

"Bit of a scoundrel though, if I'm honest."

Gerald stopped his snorting, and Leo backed up the slope at the edge of the pond and smiled. It seemed he'd put Gerald off another attack. And even better, Gerald was following him. He'd lowered his feathered shoulders, his hackles down.

Leo backed away from the pond as Gerald took to land. "Were you worried I would take her from you?" Leo sighed. "I promise that much has been resolved. She is all yours."

Leo checked over his shoulder to ensure his way to the berm was clear. When he turned back, docile Gerald was gone. In his place was a bird so ungodly tall, wings open to their maximum...

Gerald tilted his neck at Leo like a lance.

Leo ran.

He bolted across the lawn, over the berm, and toward the Nightingale pond.

The hissing followed, at various volumes and distances, but Leo did not let himself get too far ahead, for fear the bird would lose interest and turn back.

Gerald was not distracted from his chase, not even by his home pond as they came to the edge of it.

Leo stopped and, panting, relinquished himself to another pummeling from Gerald. Between rounds of blocking Gerald's bites, Leo waved frantically toward the house, begging for someone's attention.

Preferably someone who could bring the beast to heel. Only one could do that. Only April.

And that was who exited the home a moment later, approaching their chaos with complete serenity.

Leo's eyes locked with hers from behind the flurry of wings. *So calm. So smug. So beautiful. So deceitful.*

She clapped her hands gently and cooed. "Gerald, love."

The beating abated at once.

Gerald's head did not cool straight away though. He continued to make a show of his height, waddling in agitated circles as April approached.

Leo dusted himself and nodded toward his adversary. "Careful. He is possessed at present."

April's eyes widened in beautiful mock alarm. "Goodness. Not by Zeus, I hope."

Her joke drew a reluctant laugh from Leo—his heart not so fully hardened to her as he'd tried to make it.

Her eyes were not on Gerald, but on him, boring into him with cloying explanation even before she spoke.

Vulnerability to her charm was renewed the moment Leo saw that mole tick upward on her lip, the moment that sweet gap was flashed at him.

She was a five-foot giant. Capable, he knew now,

of crushing him with just a few words. He tightened his jaw... and his heart.

Gerald still circled them.

"Will you not call off your dogs?"

"Did you not boast earlier of how famously you and Gerald got along?"

"We *did* earlier." Leo insisted, dreading that she would not believe him. "I've no idea what he's at now with all this."

Gerald took one last angry lap around them before a short flight to the pond, splashing down.

"*Hmm,*" was April's response.

Leo did not appreciate her doubt. Nor did he appreciate postponement of the more pressing topic.

"Are you quite certain," started April, "that there was nothing a*fowl* with Gerald's visit to your pond today?"

Leo rolled his eyes. "Surely you secure your legacy as a great wit with lines such as that."

"I only learn from the wittiest."

Leo felt himself still under scrutiny in spite of his deflection and opted to lie about Gerald. "No, of course nothing was amiss, why would you ask such a thing?"

April shrugged. "It is only that, well, there appears to have been a struggle." She pointed beside the pond, where boot prints in the damp soil led to dual ruts in the mud—results of the dive he'd executed in capturing his prize.

April folded her hands, politely awaiting the truth like a knowing governess.

But what did he owe her? When *she* had not been truthful with *him?*

Leo shrugged. "Strange, that. For I have been home all day."

"Before going to the village."

"Before going to the village, yes."

"Where you learned something unexpected of me."

All the fight and tension went out of him at hearing the regret in her voice. "Yes," he agreed softly.

She looked straight into his eyes, baring herself completely. "I am so sorry if I have caused misunderstanding. When two persons make such a decision as that, the decision to... to..."

Leo would not let it be so implicit.

"To share their bodies within an hour of meeting?" He stepped toward her until she was forced to look up at him. He lowered his voice. "To laugh together? To fuck in a hot bath? To talk of life from morning till almost sunset?"

He sensed her lifting her foot to take a step back and caught her around the waist, but she pushed him away and darted a glance at the watchful house.

"I wronged you," she said. "I do not know what you hoped for, but I made too many assumptions and trusted it was fine to be silent based on those. I am sorry for it."

"What assumptions?"

"That an affair begun in so much haste would be ended the same. And that that is understood by all parties." She looked down, collecting herself for another thought before meeting his eye again. "I never expected to find you smiling in a shop window."

The admission eked out of her in a broken voice. It broke him the same to hear it.

"You mean you did not expect to see me at all. That you would not be *pleased* to see—"

"That is *not* what I said."

"But you are engaged! Why were you in my arms at all? You'd every chance to say it. You even called yourself 'unwed'!"

"I know!"

She cast another worried look at the house before burying her face in her hands. He thought it an act, but her hands did not come back down. Instead her soft breaths were corrupted by sobs. He gently pulled her hands away and waited for her glassy eyes to meet his.

"Why?" he asked. "That is all I wish to know." It

wasn't. He wished to know many more things, like whether it could all be undone.

"It is not what I want," said April. "But like so many brides before me, I must marry for my family's sake."

He stroked away the salty tears from her hands with his thumbs. A widow's household had few options, he knew the truth of that. Knew the commonness of April's predicament. Another feeling welled in his gut, the vague sense that he could help, mixed with the sureness of rejection.

"I'm sorry," he whispered. And he *was* sorry for her but for himself also.

"No. I'm sorry." She took her hands away from him. "You deserved to know. Forgive me." She flashed a faltering smile. "I did not expect a handsome rescuer that day."

He longed to have her hands back in his. He balled them into fists to keep from reaching for her.

"I did not expect *you*," she continued. "I did not expect that last bit of beautiful freedom and, selfishly, I took it."

That last bit of beautiful freedom. That was what he was. He squinted at the sky and nodded. Her words stung behind his eyes.

"*Oh...* No. Leo, I do not mean—"

"It is all right Miss Nightingale." The coldness of his reply was not well-hidden. He knew as much.

She tugged on his sleeve, but he could not tilt his chin down, lest the thing burning behind his eyes would come forth.

"Come. Please, Mr. Derring."

He looked down just in time to catch her eyeing the house again. It was too much.

"Stop looking over your shoulder as though this moment is the most daring we have been."

She looked again out of habit even as he said it.

"If you do not stop looking I will *give* them something to see."

Her eyes whipped back to him. He already regretted the threat, but her eyes didn't possess the expected fury.

It struck him then that his threat was not a promise of ruin but of commitment. Did she see that? Did she *want* that?

How would her eyes change if he said more? He stepped forward, and she backed against a tree. He put a hand on the trunk beside her face and made his voice as gentle as it had been.

"If you look back at that house again, April, I will take you in my arms. I will put my lips to yours and kiss you as I did in the bath. I will whisper in your ear until you melt against me. April, please."

Her lips fell softly ajar, teasing the gap in her teeth. Her chest rose and fell with long, deep breaths. Not once did her blue eyes look away.

She lifted her chin. "You willfully ignore the risks to me if we are seen. My family has been fortunate to find one who would have me."

Leo's blood curdled with the disgust that she would speak of herself so. "You would complain of your future and defend it in the same breath? What is it you *want*, April?"

"What do *you*?"

She pushed him away from her and her voice lowered to a hissing whisper. "More dalliances in your bath? More tastes of me? It goes nowhere. One day we would be found out. One day long after my last chance for marriage has passed."

"And what if someone *had* found us last week?"

"Precisely. What if someone had? It is not as though you would have married me."

She'd missed his meaning entirely. A meaning he had not yet confronted himself. An impulsive, reckless, hopeful meaning.

What if someone had? he wondered. What if in one moment they'd been sealed by scandal? What if that day had been made a lifetime?

But Leo could not bring himself to say any of it out loud. Because if she felt the same, then hope would have led her down the same foolish path. Surely April, brazen as they come, would have kissed him the moment he threatened to kiss first.

The cut of rejection was already too deep,

clouding his instincts. So his proposal remained a stone in his throat. It was not what April wished.

"You are right, Miss Nightingale. I am sorry to have troubled you."

A disturbance on the pond tore his attention away. Gerald was sniping at the swan April had paired him with.

"I see they get on as beautifully as us."

"Daphne and Gerald will be fine one day."

Leo turned back to April. "Are you sure their union is a thing that can be forced?"

April's delicate features scrunched. She put her hands on her hips and sighed, regarding her birds. She looked so confounded, but the frustration was more wistful than controlling.

"I do not know," she shrugged. "I only hope."

She gave him a weak smile. Would it be the last time he chanced upon that gap? The last time he fell into it? He started backing away before he was in too deep.

"I will leave you to your matchmaking," he nodded to the swans. "And to the match made for you. I wish you all the best."

She bade him no farewells as he turned his back, but his thoughts were rushed by words unsaid. He turned back around before she was out of earshot. She was already walking away.

"April?"

She turned.

"It was the best day of my life," he said, memorizing her.

In his dreams that night, she would say, *"Mine too."*

But here she merely nodded before continuing toward the watchful facade of the Nightingale's nest. She disappeared inside. Out of his life. Into another.

9

Leo was framed in one tiny diamond pane of the parlor window as he disappeared over the berm. A little piece of April went with him.

She laced her fingers together, trying to remember the feel of her hand in his as they tiptoed together through Derring Hall. There had been so much laughter in their eyes as they'd crouched beside tables and hid behind doors.

She imagined herself awaiting his touch in the bath... all his torturously drawn-out ministrations. Her heart kicked as she remembered the tackling and the splashing. She could still feel his breath on her ear. His chest hair between her fingers. His cock, buried inside her...

But it was still her hand in his that came easiest.

Memories of being led down rabbit-holes of youth and misadventure.

Her fingers threaded together more tightly and she closed her eyes to savor it.

"The neighbors now, April? Truly?"

April startled, whipping around to find Agatha, cross-armed in the parlor doorway.

"Ah, my favorite sister. Ever watchful of others. Ever unaware of herself."

Agatha strode in and poked at some chapbooks on the nearest table, feigning she had any purpose there other than to be a bother.

"You do not wish to scare off Mr. Gramble, do you?" she asked.

"I believe it is *you* who should be the more concerned. For upon my union with him hinges all the pretty dresses you will ever wear in the future. All the ponies your buggy will ever be drawn by. All the suitors who will demand a dowry the price of a country to take on the burden of your character."

Agatha smiled, seemingly hearing only the truth of the correction and dismissing its insult. And why should she not be happy? When April's suffering would bring heroic amounts of coin to their coffer.

"See that you do not allow our futures to slip through that gap of yours, dear sister." She flicked her tongue at her own front teeth before recovering a smug smile.

With that, she slithered off. April shut the door behind her and sank against it.

"The best day of my life," she whispered, to none but herself.

That was what he'd said. But how could that be when he had traveled to faraway lands and been raised on an estate four times the size of her family's own? In fact, several generations back, the Nightingale parcel had *belonged* to the Derring line. It was only granted to them as part of a knighthood awarded to April's great-grandfather.

Perhaps in a different time, in a different place...

She frowned.

She had freely given up that information which was most lackluster about her. She had teased about her ill reputation because a tryst had been her only aim. And how was she to secure it without first expressing a fervent openness to it? For the first time, she worried her impulse had spoiled something. Not by being any worse than previous impulses, but by way of there being something to spoil.

The best day of my life. The more she repeated those words in her mind, the more she felt the statement to be mutual. She'd not have sacrificed that day with Leo. She'd not have given it up to play a longer game or be someone different. At least that was some comfort.

His words still pestered her as the windows darkened and the desk's candle was lit. As she sat to write her menu...

Seed cakes
Clotted cream
A bowl of peaches
A bowl of ~~more peaches~~

She stared numbly at her list. Hothouse peaches would cost a fortune this time of year. A half an hour came and went. She crumpled the paper. Marjorie, their kitchen maid, would have to make the rest up when she went to fetch things. She was better at it anyhow.

April looked up from the desk, expecting a view of the berm, before remembering it was dark and she had moved upstairs to her bedchamber. There was no view of Derring Hall from her corner of the house.

A frisson of anxiety shot through her. How would she sleep knowing Mr. Gramble arrived in the morning? Knowing she'd have mere hours to converse with him before family and acquaintances arrived for tea? And then a wedding... and then...

She prayed he would not show. Perhaps his coach would be set upon by thieves? *No. Too cruel a thought.* Perhaps... perhaps a band of terribly marriageable ladies who go wet at the thought of shrewd old importers instead? *Yes. That would see everyone happy.*

April's bedchamber overlooked the pond. There, two white spots floated at opposite ends beneath the moonlight. She opened the window and rested her elbows on the sill.

Gerald will come 'round to Daphne, she thought. *They will mate for life and be happy.*

Someone had to end up happy. The longer she stared at the swans, the more certain she was that that someone would not be her.

Worry roiled within her as tears pricked the back of her eyes. She sniffed them back as a breeze whisked through the window. The night air was crisp. Invigorating. Hopeful, even?

She took a bracing breath as a surge of impulsiveness—that trait which was so a part of her—took hold.

She did not even pause to don slippers as she stormed from the bedchamber...

Anna had successfully coerced April into lavender ribbons for the tea. But before her pathetic menu could be laid out—peach bowl and all—she would face the formal introduction to her betrothed, Mr. Gramble.

She longed to wait for him outside where she

might better breathe, but Mama insisted, as she often did, on something more orchestrated.

"I can see your skirts, darling!" called Mama from the foot of the stairs.

April tucked herself around the hall corner, clinging to the papered wall as though a murderer was lurking.

"That is better. Now remember, count to ten with long, slow breaths once I call you down. You must keep your future husband in breathless suspense!"

April rolled her eyes. Was it not *she* who was in breathless suspense? And was it not she who would perish from it?

She'd been directed to her position nearly half an hour ago. It was the culmination of a mere thirty days since Mr. Gramble had formally offered for her in a letter. The creatures fluttering in her stomach had turned to beasts and were surely eating her alive.

"He arrives!" The squeal came from Anna who had eagerly been playing sentry at the attic window.

The lavender sash in April's hair felt suddenly too tight.

Moments later, Anna scurried down the corridor. April caught her by the arm.

"You've a cobweb." April plucked the sticky gray attic remnant from her sister's brunette curls.

She expected Anna to hurry off, but her sister

paused. Anna's heart-shaped cheeks were were high and smiling, but her hazel eyes were full of concern.

"You are helping all of us. I know that, and I am so grateful to call you a sister." Anna lunged then, flinging both arms around April.

April did her best to return the embrace despite her arms being pinned.

"I love you," muttered Anna into April's shoulder.

"I love you too." April rubbed her sister's back. It did help to know her sacrifice was not in vain.

Anna pulled away. "Mr. Gramble will be wonderful. I'm sure of it."

Of that, April was less certain, but she braved a smile as Anna heeded a call from their mother to get downstairs.

April took a deep breath as she heard the entry door downstairs being opened. Why did the world not intervene? Was she to be handed over to a new life without so much as a hiccup of protest from the universe?

The night before, she had crept from the house in bare feet and tossed Gerald over the berm. Had tossed him like a wish. Where was her answer to that wish?

Her mother's voice went up in pitch as she greeted their guest downstairs.

"Mr. Gramble. How good of you to come all this way."

"Travel is hardly an undertaking when my bride awaits."

He, at least, did not sound so very old for his age. There were more polite murmurs before the call to action came:

"Mr. Gramble, it is my pleasure to present you with my eldest, Miss April Nightingale."

April closed her eyes and began to count on deep breaths. *One. Two. Three...* She swayed queasily... *Eight. Nine—*

She opened her eyes, ready to twirl into view at the top of the stairs, but Agatha was right there.

"What are you about? You look ridiculous," she hissed, obliviously jostling past April to start down the stairs herself.

"No! Agatha! You have spoiled—" Her mother's manners recovered. "My apologies, Mr. Gramble."

April turned the corner, hoping to rescue her mother from her fluster.

"April! You must—no!" Mama hand-waved her back into place but it was too late. April had laid eyes on Mr. Gramble and was too intrigued by the chaos to reverse course.

Agatha proceeded down the stairs ahead of her at a tortoise's pace. In the entry was a straight-backed gentleman with a hat under his arm and head of thick silver hair. He did not spare a glance for April but carefully studied Agatha's descent.

Mama swirled her fingers at her temples before yanking a bewildered Agatha from the bottom step. "Mr. Gramble, forgive me. This is my middle daughter, Agatha. And this—" She gestured up toward April with an encouraging smile. "And this beauty of mine is Miss April, your betrothed."

Mr. Gramble finally looked up. The sketched portrait he had sent ahead of him was unflattering in the face of reality, adding deep lines to his face where he only had the standard creases of expression. His silver hair swept elegantly forward and was peppered with remnants of a dark brown. Not so terrible, in all fact. The portraitist did, however, capture his ears— his rather prominent ears—with accuracy.

He put a hand over his heart and bowed, extending a hand to assist April from the final steps. "Miss Nightingale, I have long awaited our meeting. You are as elegant as promised."

"Mr. Gramble." April smiled and dipped in a curtsy but had no words for him in return. For though he did not offend her, compliments felt as inaccessible as the stars.

10

Leo woke before dawn, tortured by an overconsumption of brandy the night before.

Tomorrow she will be wed. Gone.

He staggered down the hall and heard his father's bell. But Partridge was not in sight. He sighed and entered the darkened room.

"Is that you, Partridge?"

"It is Leo."

"Ah! You are up early."

Leo's eyes adjusted to the darkness. His father was not in bed but in his usual chair by a dwindling fire.

"I wonder if you might rescue me from all these blankets? Eliza must have crept in in the night. She will smother me to death one day."

"She is only trying to do her job well."

Eliza, a chambermaid, had been promoted to Mr. Derring's caregiver and had seized on it with much devotion.

"I know it."

Leo unburied his father from a full stack of coverlets. "Does this mean you will stretch your legs today?"

"If I do not, I will become one with the chair."

Leo smiled and helped his father up. The elder Derring unfolded to a height very near his own. His nose flinched as they came eye to eye.

"Have you been drinking this morning?"

Leo looked down at himself, at least he had a proper coat on.

"Not this morning but last night. Never mind it."

His father leaned on him for a few faltering steps before finding his feet and walking away toward his wall of atlases. "You only drink when there is a reason to. So what was it?"

"A social occasion," said Leo.

His father looked over his shoulder and gave him a wilted look. "You are a poor liar, even when sober."

Leo watched him from across the room, resisting the urge to rush and help him with the heavy book he was pulling from a high shelf. His father could still do plenty for himself and ought to be left to do so.

His father was the only person Leo had in the world now that his years of travel were over.

A little door in Leo's heart cracked open. "It is a woman," he admitted.

The atlas Isambard had been reaching for tipped into his hand, dropping his elbow with its weight. He turned around, a lopsided smile on his weathered face.

"Oh?" was all he said, doing poorly to hide his obvious interest. "I did not realize you had been out much."

"I've not. In truth, I came across her here."

His father raised both eyebrows and went to the desk to set down his chosen book. He took a seat in a velvet chair and opened the tome, an atlas. Leo had acquired his love of cartography from his father, who admired maps as a pastime.

"You have told me many stories from your time abroad, my son, but this one is starting off far more interesting." He leaned back. "Please go on."

"A few days back we had a trespasser, struggling to retrieve a waterfowl gone astray in our pond."

"She came to fetch a duck?"

"The unmarked swan, actually."

"Oh, but I love that swan."

The earnest lilt of his father's admission drew a laugh from Leo. "Then you already have something in common with our swan-obsessed trespasser."

His father looked toward the distant window, his brows pinched.

"Worry not, our swan still resides here. It was another that she meant to take."

"And what then?" asked his father.

"She got herself in a spot of trouble by falling into our pond."

The elder Derring pursed his lips and shrugged his shoulders in a chuckle. "Ah, well then. I am sure what you did next was *very* proper."

Leo had no desire to see his father's brow raise any higher. "Never mind the details. She left with her swan."

"Eventually?"

Leo sighed. "Eventually."

Mr. Derring licked a finger and turned the atlas' page. "I take it this swan had not flown too far?"

"Just over the berm."

That got his father's *full* attention.

"A Nightingale girl?"

Leo nodded, eager to learn what his father knew. He approached the desk. "What do you know of Mrs. Nightingale and her daughters?"

His father was suddenly coy, despite revealing his interest. He shrugged. "I know only that Mr. Nightingale passed not long after the third girl was born..." Mr. Derring put on his spectacles and darted a bashful glance toward his son. "And that Mrs. Nightingale was, for a few years, set on remarrying to the widower next door."

Leo slammed both hands to his father's desk, leaning on it. "No," he breathed, delighting in the rarity of gossip from his old man.

He waited for his father to look up again. When he did, he wore an impish grin. "You may think me vain in saying so, but she did not hide it."

"What did she do?"

"She would sit upon the back end of the berm and watch me prune Lisbeth's roses. She'd wave whenever she caught my eye, but it was really the sitting that most gave her away, that and the way she ate fruit."

"How did she eat fruit?"

His father thought a moment. "Carnally?"

"Say no more." Leo truly did not wish to hear the details. "But Mrs. Nightingale is a handsome woman for her age, is she not?"

"Her handsomeness was not the problem, nor was her character, which I found quite charming. It was that I was still tending your mother's rose garden along with my broken heart. It was too soon. I could not bear Mrs. Nightingale's fawning, but it was never personal."

Leo's own heart tightened. The rose garden which had kept the spirit of his mother alive had not been looked after in two years, not since the old man's energy had begun to dwindle.

"Personal or not, I worry she may have taken it that way."

"That is a shame then, and I hope I will have the chance to remedy it." Isambard propped his elbow on the desk and rested his weary head. "Just when did you chance to meet the widow?"

"The same day I learned her trespassing daughter was betrothed."

"Oh son, I'm so sorry."

Leo averted his eyes from his father's pitying pout.

"Keep heart, Leo. These things break off all the time."

Leo nodded in acknowledgment, deciding not to share that the wedding itself happened on the morrow. He began to pace.

"Will you sit and tell me more?"

Leo felt a tug toward the chair his father gestured to, but he writhed at the idea of his pain being the thing of focus.

"I think it best if I take my moping, and my headache, back to my room."

His father leaned forward and flipped more frantically through the atlas in front of him at the threat of Leo's departure. Leo leaned forward to see what his father was getting at, but it looked like any regular atlas.

Its uniqueness was proven a moment later when

his father let out a surprisingly robust *"Aha!"* Leo was waved around to his father's side of the desk, and a folded paper, plucked from the book's crease, was handed to him.

"We saved this. Your mother and I."

Leo reached out for the little paper, not recognizing it. Unfolding it, he found the uneven scrawl of a child and a series of lines. He peeked over the document at his father, whose thrilled expression did nothing to solve the puzzle of what he held.

"Do you not recognize your own hand?" His father laughed.

Leo looked back at the paper and saw it then. Little memories sprang forth to color the page. It was the first map he had ever drawn. It depicted the Derring lawns. The pond. The berm. An arrow leaping over the berm to a large "X" marking a treasure.

"You were our little pirate, so convinced there was treasure over there."

Leo traced his thumb to the X in the page's corner, breathing an unsteady breath. "Did I know the Nightingale girls?"

"You ran about with them a time or two. I wish I could tell you more, but my garret is a bit fusty these days." Mr. Derring tapped his temple.

Leo passed the map back to his father.

"You do not wish to keep it?"

"No, but thank you for showing me." Leo backed toward the door, his headache, suddenly more piercing.

"I know, I know. You have moping to do. You should do it outside and get some air. It will be good for your headache."

It sounded, in fact, like the *least* good thing for his headache. "You talk as though you do not hide in here all day." Leo swerved toward the nearest window on his way out and tore open its drapes. The soft light of a spring morning flooded the corner, being both very beautiful and very assaulting to his tender senses at once. He turned back to his father who was scowling, squinting like a mole in the intrusive beam.

"You know, father. It is not too late in the year to prune the roses." It was, in fact, too late in the year, but Leo hoped he might consider it anyhow.

Once outside, Leo was pleased to look up and see his father had not shut the drapes again.

He was displeased, however, by just about everything else. The sunshine was anything but a cure for the vengeance of brandy.

Decades ago, he'd marked the Nightingale land with an X. He strained to remember whether he knew any of the girls then? Anna would not yet have been born. April, being nearest in age to him, was by far the most likely. Had they sneaked through a house together back then? Had they played hide-and-find as little ones?

He would expel from mind every memory of his travels, if only to remember better the age of six. He could not say why he'd drawn the X there. He only knew that now, two dozen years later, it felt very right. For there, on the other side of the berm was a treasure.

His ruminations brought him back to the edge of the pond, to the best grove of trees to shade him from the punishing sun. He sat down and rested his back against an ash. The pile of dredged up mud festered nearby in the sun, lending an unsweet odor to the area. Like so much else, it suited the mood.

He pinched his eyes shut against a wave of head spins and rested.

At least, he did until a series of squeaks and snorts broke the air. He sighed. Mute swans, for their name, could make an awful lot of racket.

He opened one eye, expecting to see the wild swan nearby, but what he witnessed was something unexpectedly more energetic.

Gerald was in the water on *top* of the unmarked swan. He slid off of her and they both made a ritual of dunking their heads beside one another, before coming back up together, necks crossed. Then Gerald would attempt to mount again.

To Leo's horrified eyes, the cob succeeded,

wiggling his tail and pushing the wild swan's head underwater as he did his natural business. It seemed, for a moment, like something to be intervened in, like something that could go horribly wrong, but Leo reminded himself that he and April had made quite a messy ritual of the act themselves.

Things quieted down some and Leo's unease turned into awe as the birds continued to dip their heads in rhythm.

They came up again and Gerald's long, elegant neck was hooked with that of the wild pen. Time slowed down. The birds floated cheek to cheek.

It was the very thing April had described. It was her dream. Her wish.

Was it so terrible that it was not Daphne whom Gerald had mated with? Would it not please April to see the creature settled happily?

A flood of urgency carried Leo away from his headache. He was consumed instead by the certainty that he had to tell April. He had to share this with her, had to show her Gerald linking necks with his mate, contented.

He ran to the berm but stopped short before coming down its other side.

Small clusters of strangers filtered in and out of the Nightingale house. His chest tightened as he remembered: the tea. The one April's youngest sister had made mention of. The one she had *invited* him to.

Leo straightened his coat and descended the berm at a more dignified pace.

Daphne floated alone on the Nightingale pond, seemingly unbothered that her pre-selected mate was tupping the pen next door.

The home welcomed Leo with a surprisingly bright and cheerful ground floor. The walls were painted a pale blue that, considering signs of age, still drew sunshine into every corner.

He entered a salon dotted with an eclectic assortment of chairs, doubtless borrowed from the rest of the house. Cheerful vignettes dotted the room where visitors had pulled their seats into little circles. Cups and saucers rested on laps and the gentle murmur of polite conversation filled the space. A round table with a smattering of tea cakes—and a bowl of peaches, for some reason—was the room's centerpiece.

April, however, could not be seen.

"Mr. Derring?" The voice was Mrs. Nightingale's and was unambiguously disapproving.

Leo armed himself with a put-on smile as he turned to the matriarch. There was some relief when he saw young Anna at her side.

"Do not be cross, Mama. I invited him, remember?"

The elder Nightingale did not condone his presence verbally but dipped her head in tight-lipped acknowledgment.

Leo dipped his in kind, but could not resist a bit of troublemaking in light of recent discoveries. "Mrs. Nightingale, thank you for having me. My father sends his *fond* regards."

Her eyes widened but not angrily. She leaned forward, suddenly welcoming of more conversation.

"Oh? And where is your father today?"

"I did not see it fitting to extend my invitation any further than it might already be stretched," he shot a quick smile at Anna. "Besides, I'd have loved if he could join us here but I know there is tension between you, and he keeps mostly to his rooms besides."

Mrs. Nightingale nodded. "It is true that I do not see him outside much of late." Her face grew more serious, schooling any hint of eagerness. "As for the prior, I can be forgiving."

"He will be pleased to hear that. And he would be out more, but he ailed this winter."

Mrs. Nightingale's expression changed entirely as she brought one hand to her lips to hide a gasp. "Ailed? Why did he not send word that he was poorly?!"

She was suddenly so animated with worry that she nearly grabbed Leo's wrist. Her hand hovered there a moment before she self-corrected. She was a far cry from the steely woman he had met in the shop.

The matron's lacy cap slipped slightly forward and she readjusted it, taking a moment to rein in her look of concern. She folded her hands. "I am sorry to hear my neighbor is unwell. For all our disagreement, I do not wish that upon him. We'd have extended our help in any way had we known."

"I am sure he will regret he did not send word."

"We'd have sent him many baskets." She said, a hitch detectable in her voice. "Will he be all right?" A hand shot to her lips again. "Please say he is not on his deathbed. That is not why you are back in Dorset, I hope?"

Leo reassured her with a smile and a shake of his head. "My father is getting on in years, of course, but he is far from that. I do wish he would get outside though. It would help his strength."

"Then I wish he would as well. I miss seeing him tend his roses."

Leo smiled, feeling something should be gently clarified. "Do you know they were actually my mother's roses?"

Mrs. Nightingale nervously twisted a handful of her skirt. "I did not."

"I think my father has not had the heart to see to them in a long time."

Mrs. Nightingale nodded; her mouth was turned down in a guilty pout. Leo wished she would not feel such a way over a mere misunderstanding.

"I hope you will see him out there again one day soon."

"Me too," she said.

Before the woman grew too lost in memory, Leo had to ask after his purpose there: "Where is Miss April?"

The matriarch raised an eyebrow and Leo hastened to ease any suspicion.

"I must congratulate her and give her my well wishes." It took more courage to say those words than to sail across the North Atlantic. Yet somehow, he'd uttered them convincingly enough to receive Mrs. Nightingale's direction to the adjoining room. And he *did* wish, truly, in that moment, for April to have the best. The best life. The best marriage. And the great solace of seeing her swan dance with its mate.

"She will be by the corner windows, becoming better acquainted with her betrothed."

Leo thanked Mrs. Nightingale and began to walk, suddenly wondering whether he was prepared to find her.

Better acquainted with her betrothed. Leo's body ached against those words. One such as April should not have to settle for one she had just become acquainted with. Leo noted the snag in his logic and laughed at himself. April was no more acquainted with him than with her fiancé. If they had felt what they felt after one day, there was nothing in the rules of life that could prevent the same from happening with another.

He entered the dining room and saw them by the windows, April and, presumably, her betrothed. The man had a head of silver hair, but his features were upsettingly fine.

April sat neatly in a straight-backed dining chair. White muslin spilled over her knees and the tail of a lavender sash in her hair spilled like water over one shoulder. Elbows in at her sides, she operated in a narrow space, lifting her teacup primly to her lips. She gave Mr. Gramble her full attention, but her smile was tight, disallowing the man any glimpses of that precious gap.

At the risk of interrupting, Leo opted to wait and be noticed.

At last her eyes drifted past Mr. Gramble's shoulder, and up, and up...

Leo could not help but smile as their eyes met, however doleful he felt inside.

The same smile did not come to hers. But it tried. The broken-winged flutter at one corner of her lips told him how she tried.

It was acknowledgment enough for him to step in. "Apologies, for my interruption."

Leo's words ran over the last vestiges of Mr. Gramble's story about a shipment that did not make it to Calais on time. The man, unaware of his presence till then, turned at the waist to regard Leo behind him.

April set down her cup and stood. "Mr. Gramble, may I introduce Mr. Derring? Mr. Derring is our neighbor to the west."

Mr. Gramble acknowledged Leo without getting up. "Mr. Derring."

"Mr. Gramble."

The silence stretched uncomfortably long when Leo was not invited to join them.

Leo tried not stare but it was dreadful difficult tearing his eyes from April's. There was too much he wanted to know about what he saw there. The fluttering hint of a smile was gone, replaced by something nearer to dread. Did she worry he was there to humiliate her?

"I only come to wish you glad as a couple and to—"

"We are grateful for your well wishes," said Gramble. If you will excuse us though, we were—"

"I also have news for Miss Nightingale."

Mr. Gramble's attention whipped toward his wife-to-be.

April floundered under their dual gazes. "I...

perhaps we ought to... if you will pardon me Mr. Gramble, I—"

The man turned back to Leo. "What news?"

Leo had hoped to succeed in getting April away from Mr. Gramble to tell her, but it was probably for the best he did not. There was no telling the impulsiveness of his heart in the absence of spectators.

Still, as soon as he began to speak, she became the only person in the room and Mr. Gramble, an afterthought. Leo swept toward her on one knee—never having been offered a chair—and told her with great excitement what he'd seen.

"Gerald has mated and is cheek to cheek with his mate even as we speak. It is the most beautiful dance, just as you had hoped for." He thought a moment and corrected. "Well, it is not *all* beauty. A bit vicious, if I'm honest."

April very nearly spilled her tea, so frantic she was to set it down.

Her fluttering smile took flight and she flashed that gap at him, matching his excitement measure for measure. Mr. Gramble had, apparently, disappeared for her as well.

"They are together? Gerald and Daphne?" April looked past his shoulder as though she could see straight through the walls to the pond if she tried hard enough.

"Well, here is the thing—"

"Careful making her smile too much, Mr. Derring. She has a trench there one might trip into." Mr. Gramble tapped his own front teeth with a fingernail and smiled at April as though this was a joke she loved—something they had shared for ages.

"Oh, I have fallen into it before." Leo's mouth ran ahead of common sense, but he did not regret it.

Mr. Gramble shifted in his seat but retained a tight smile. "And what did you find there, Mr. Derring?"

As her future husband, you should know, Leo wished to say. Instead he answered, "A spirited heart."

"Not *too* spirited, let us hope."

April did not even wince at her husband's offhand disregard. And Leo was fortunate to still be basking in her smile.

She was precisely the sort of "spirited" that was an insult in their circles. It brought Leo joy to see her unashamed of it.

"What were you saying about the swans?" she asked. "Shall we go out and see them?"

Mr. Gramble stood then, dwarfing both of them in their hunched, conspiratorial positions. He wore a surprisingly game smile, all things considered. "Would one be so kind as to shed light on this conversation for me?"

April stood, as did Leo, and she began to explain.

"It is about swans. You see, I have two swans, Gerald and Daphne, one of which I raised from hatching."

Mr. Gramble cocked his head and pouted slightly. "Your family has the privilege of Swan Marks?" He took a sip from a dainty glass in his hand and turned to Leo to share a skeptical expression. Leo did not join him in it. Rather, he indulged in the sight of April as she came to her own defense, chin up.

"I will have you know, Mr. Gramble, that this family has had the honor for several generations. My great-grandfather was a physician to the nobility and was granted Swan Marks when this land was passed to him. Most of the original flock's lineage is gone now. Gerald is the last of the line and it is my mission to reinvigorate it. I wish to see him mate and be happy." April turned to Leo then, seemingly trying to bring an increasingly impassioned speech back under her control. "They mate for life, you know."

Leo was astonished. Her obsession with Gerald and Daphne was no longer merely charming but noble. All along, she had been trying to save something of her family's. And things had not quite gone as planned. Leo dreaded to tell her, but:

"I must make one small correction."

April's smile brightened, not anticipating anything dire. And indeed it was not dire... was it?

"It is not Daphne who is with Gerald."

Her smile plummeted. Dire, it was.

"You mean he is with the wrong swan?"

At that, a gauntlet was thrown down. "*Wrong* swan? There is nothing the matter with my swan. Gerald has merely followed his heart."

April laughed, and a whistle inadvertently escaped her little gap, inflaming her further.

"His *heart*? You speak of Gerald's heart? He is a *bird*."

Leo scoffed and closed the space between them, heedless of her fiancé.

"Strange for that to rankle you when you would lose your shoes and dignity in the mud before seeing him 'in love' in the wrong pond."

"Your swan is a wild, untamed thing."

"The king should hear you speak of his royal birds so. Besides, I do not think swans much care about one another's upbringing when they do these things." Leo thought back to the violence of the birds' passion. "Gerald certainly didn't."

April's eyes went wide as she pointed her nose in the air and seethed. He grinned, pleased that he had crossed a line.

The fire was back in her eyes. He watched as rebellious insults crossed her expression and burnt out like little embers. This was the April he knew. The April he *loved*.

And he would gladly provoke her for more of it. "Gerald comes over the berm of his own free will and has found love in my pond."

"Except he did not. Not this time, because I—"

Leo cocked his head. "You what?"

She stopped herself from saying it, but it was too late. He knew. Knew what she had done, even without her answer.

She spun to her betrothed, "Mr. Gramble, please excuse..." But the apology fell on empty space. Mr. Gramble was now across the room, absorbed into a small circle of shocked onlookers helmed by her sister, Agatha. A circle of raised brows.

It did not go unnoticed by Leo that Mr. Gramble's hand hovered briefly at the small of Agatha's back. Leo did not like the man.

"Well, you got your wish," said April. "A private audience with me."

Leo felt the eyes of the whole room on them. "Not really the sort of privacy we're accustomed to."

April lowered her voice. "You should not be here."

"I was invited by your young sister, Anna, if you recall."

April crossed her arms.

He knew his invitation did not exactly fall within the bounds of legitimacy. "Trust that I secured your mother's blessing on arrival."

April lowered her voice in a way mismatched to the flames in her eyes.

"And you have come to what? To change my mind? To preserve our affair? To take me to some nook where we might have a final go at it?"

The tang of her words was acid against his heart, against his *true* intentions.

"No. I came here to tell you about a bird. To share news that I thought would bring you joy before your wedding day."

He looked around the room, trying to avoid the heartbreaking sight of her gaze, trying to find the words to sting her back.

"I came to tell you of a bird. A bird in *love*. However..." He took a long, steadying breath but could not help himself from one last provocation: "If you know of such a nook, April..."

Her blue eyes unfocused. She no longer looked at him but through him, seemingly stunned. It gave him leave to memorize her eyes, the dark ring around an aquamarine iris, pupils that were ever-shifting when she was lost in thought. He looked one final time at her slack, speechless lips... at the mole... the gap...

Then he straightened his coat and walked away. He felt her gaze burning on his back as he walked straight to Mr. Gramble's circle. "Forgive my prior intrusion. I merely wished to alert Miss Nightingale to her wayward swan. A pet she cares for very much."

Mr. Gramble shrugged. "The sort of triviality I am sure marriage will cure her of. Besides, she will be bringing no pets to my estate, of that you can be certain. I cannot focus on my business knowing beasts are ruining the house while I am away."

"And are you away much, Mr. Gramble?"

"Constantly."

"May I ask what business you are in?"

"Sugar and spices, mostly."

"A high cost in that trade, is there not?"

"'Tis *very* lucrative."

It was the high *human* cost of which Leo spoke. But Mr. Gramble's gray eyes glittered like the coins in his coffers.

Agatha joined the fray. "You will keep the swan, won't you, Mr. Derring? We do not want it back. Anna is not the only one who has been bit."

"The swan will remain wherever it prefers to be as far as I am concerned."

"I vow that it prefers to be *faaar* away from here." Agatha smirked.

Mr. Gramble seemed to hang on her words, a smile cutting across his sharp jaw. Without shame, Agatha batted her lashes at him.

Leo's head spun, and he caught himself on his heel before walking away from the little group. With no lovely Nightingale to distract him, his headache returned in full force. He went to the table at the center of the front room and took a peach for himself. Finding a quiet corner, he sat to nurse his headache and his hopes.

The Nightingales' guests fell calmly back into circles of soft, delighted musings, forgetting he had ever instigated a public scene with his beautiful neighbor.

But it was less his headache than his words that held him back from leaving. His final words to her had not merely been meant to provoke—they were an earnest invitation. A *coward's* invitation. He stared ruefully at the archway to the dining room. Would she accept?

He'd lied to himself. He *had* come with motives beyond sharing news of the swans. He had seen meaning in their ritual—particularly in Gerald's choosing of the "wrong" swan. He longed for April to see it too.

11

If you know of such a nook...

Leo's words repeated themselves over and over in April's mind, as persistent as the mating calls of a songbird... and just as effective.

April tried to listen to a well-wisher as they droned on through their interminable anecdote. But Leo's words still intruded.

If you know of such a nook...

Let's see, thought April. There was the spot behind the bookcases, where old shelves had been torn out. There was the musty corner of the pantry. The unused crawl space under the eave. But least frequented, and most nookish of all, was the closet to the unused servant's stairs. The door always jammed shut in a way that made everyone assume it was locked. It was cobwebbed and dark. The perfect hole to crawl into for one feeling similarly neglected. Or for two.

April had worried Leo was gone before finally spotting him in the corner of the front room, slumped like a rag in the least comfortable armchair. Her more curious relations strayed near him, only to laugh politely before being repelled by his sardonic and melancholy state.

And what need had he to be so melancholy? The loss of the mistress that April refused to be to him? The harsh thought dissolved as she looked at him... at the truth of him.

Dejected in the corner, she did not see a greedy man, nor a rake. Nor did she recall a single ill feeling when his hand had been around hers. He had been light. Light and loving. And now he was withered with a distant gaze. Like a poet seeking the words for... for heartache? *He cannot possibly feel so strongly.*

Yet he had come to her with the eager brightness of a child, to gush over the very thing she had been so excited by herself. Two swans in love.

Leo flinched and April hurried to look away. Her eyes landed on Mr. Gramble.

Her future husband stood beside Agatha with one hand hovering too-solicitously near her lower back as they laughed together. Whatever it was they laughed about, it could not be so pure and wonderful as all the laughter at Derring Hall.

The feeling of superiority was short-lived, because Leo was no longer laughing. And neither was she.

If you know of such a nook...

Her eyes looked back to the corner and Leo was gone. She looked around frantically. *Where had he—?*

There was a sigh of relief as she spotted him with Anna and her mother. The hand over his heart and apologetic smile, however, told her he was making his farewells.

And just as the night before, when April had tossed a large bird over the berm, she let her silly heart take charge.

She hurried to the letter desk, abandoning the aunt whose story she had long-ceased listening to. She removed her glove and tapped the quill on her tongue before dipping it. Within seconds she had scrawled her note:

Do not leave. Go to back of house. Back stairs are across from second east window. Door will be cracked.

She lingered behind her mother and sister, needing to catch Leo's attention. At last he turned his tortured gaze on her. When she was sure he would not look away, she turned to speak to someone and wiggled the note behind her back.

A telling hopelessness bore down on her as she waved the little flag of surrender behind her. Her heart beat faster and faster. As fast as it had during a stealthy trip through Derring Hall but now with truer stakes. She realized then that her heart was laid out to be broken. That it truly belonged to someone. To Leo.

Her fingers itched to feel him take the note. But his voice behind her, and any sign of his gentle farewells, faded. Her mother wandered into sight. As did Anna. And she imagined Leo crossing the threshold. Going home.

Her heart bottomed out, and the room became a blur. She drew the note into her palm, crumpling it. At least she had been brave. At least she had tried. Had dared. She smiled and nodded along to a new conversation, but she had to get away. Had to escape to her chosen nook and be alone with her regret.

She put a hand on the arm of the nearest guest. "If you will pardon me, I feel suddenly queasy. I must seek some water."

Even her own words were deadened by a sudden blanket of sorrow as she teetered away.

The murmurs of the entire ground floor became a hum as she stepped back to flee.

But she backed into something, *someone*, familiar. She would know the feel of his body even at the most fleeting touch.

She spun. "Leo. You are still here?"

"Leaving," he said. "But I could not go without giving you my best."

He lifted her hand—accurately choosing the one with the note. And as he pulled it to his lips for a kiss, he scraped the ball of paper from her palm into his.

His lips branded her skin with the promise that her note would be read. But would it be welcomed?

He lowered her hand partway but did not let go.

"I wish you a true happiness, Miss Nightingale. May you live like a swan with your chosen one."

There was no edge to his words, but they cut her just the same. He *meant* it. He wished her to be happy. He concluded with a sad smile that she recognized as genuine. She returned it, making sure to show him the gap that he'd made such ado about.

He bowed and departed, carrying all her hope on his coattails.

Minutes later, she was tucked onto the back stairs in the dark, waiting to either nurse her wounds or be ravaged in the arms of a neighborly man.

Her shoulders jumped as the sliver of light from the cracked door became a wide pane across her face. The silent shadow looming in the gap was Leo's.

"You must pull it shut quite firmly," she said.

Wordlessly, he did, and they were cloaked in perfect silence and darkness. A time for whispers.

"This is the best nook I have to offer," she said.

"I assure you, it is *not*." Leo's hand found her upper thigh in total darkness and gave it a squeeze through her frock.

Warmth rushed to her cheeks. She had expected her nervousness to dissolve. Instead, it was kindled in a way very unlike anything she had ever felt.

She reached up and felt in the dark until she found his sleeve. She guided him down over her as she leaned back against the jutting steps. She felt him place a knee on the step between her legs.

"Why did you bring me here, April?" he whispered.

"This time is our last."

Leo's silence merged with the darkness.

April pushed herself to say more. "Do you..." she hesitated, "...knowing it is the last, would you still want to—"

Somehow his lips found hers with flawless accuracy, prying her mouth gently open. His tongue glided once across her teeth before opening her up to him, prying deeper and deeper.

And then he pulled away.

"April, I will adhere to your wishes with religious fervor. Thank you for telling me what I must understand to consent to this, but now I must do the same."

Her body rejected the seriousness of his whisper, and she had to brave a cold pit in her stomach to respond to him.

"What must I understand?" she asked.

"You must know that I want so much more."

Her body tensed, but she did her best to be honest. "That frightens me."

"Why April?" The darkness spoke so gently above her.

"Because I do not wish to cause you pain."

"You think it causes me pain to know I will never touch you again?"

His question sounded like some sort of trick, yet there was nothing but patience in his voice. "I... yes, I suppose I do."

"You are not wrong." Leo kissed her forehead, her eyelid, every spot he could find besides her lips. "That is a thing that hurts me. But it is not that which destroys me."

April's heart beat faster and her skin tingled where he'd kissed her. "Destroys you? What destroys you?"

"The loss of that day together. That day which saw such large smiles on both our faces. That day which will never be repeated."

April had mourned that day too. The difference was, she had gone into it with mourning. Had gone into knowing what he did not know. What she had kept from him.

"I was terrible for not being clear with my intentions."

"I understand why you were not. I understand you need something more in life than to be one's mistress. I understand why your intentions would be guarded, as those of men so often are. After all, I did not clarify my intentions either. What I do not understand, though, is how you do not see it now?"

"How I do not...?" April did not know what she ought to see. She could, quite literally, not see at all.

"April Nightingale, I would *marry* you."

It all happened at once, a surge of oblivion as his meaning sank in, the feel of his body pressing down against her in the dark, the lip of a stair cutting into her back, pinching off her mind from all good sense.

"But we have only had one day."

"Is that not one day better than you have had with your fiancé?"

A tangled life of rules unbraided itself before her eyes. She had so long prided herself on eschewing etiquette, yet had somehow still been adhering to its cruelest constraints. She had known a man for one day and had fallen in love. She had tried not to see it, because it did not fit some plan. Of her mother's. Of her sister's. Of her own.

She rose to find Leo's lips and bumped his chin

instead. In doing so, she lit the same fuse of chaos that had been sparked in their bath.

His hands covered her in the dark, feeling like a dozen moving over her all at once. His mouth surprised her, falling hot through the layers of muslin over her breast. Together, they pulled up her skirts.

Leopold Derring's mouth fell hot on her again... this time much lower, and she barely remembered not to shriek. She reached down and threaded her fingers into his dark waves.

His mouth covered her quim, and he began lapping her like honey. She bit into her wrist to stifle groans of pleasure. The sensation was so surprising, so explicit, so focused in the absence of light, that her body tried to escape it. But she knew better than her body, and she clutched at Leo's hair, holding him tight to his torturous work. She could bear it.

She did not tire of his mouth—would *never*—but she needed more. A distinct tug of his hair snatched him from his open-mouthed ministrations.

"I need you," she whispered, "I need the rest of you. I cannot rest until I am full of you. And even here in the dark, I will know if you spare even an inch of yourself from me."

"Unthinkable," he whispered. A sated growl preceded the reshuffling of limbs.

Some part of Leo struck the stairwell's wainscoting. They froze, holding their breaths as they awaited any sign of commotion beyond the door.

"You must be more careful," April cautioned.

"Nonsense. I am as graceful as a swan." Leo proved it by deftly finding her thigh and stroking it to the knee, before guiding her to wrap her leg around him. "Can you see me at all?"

"No."

"Good. I cannot see you either, but I can feel you, April Nightingale. I can feel the heat between your hips. And I know precisely where your quim awaits me."

The sensual threat in his words unmade her. The staircase ascended above them, yet was a dark abyss to be fallen into rather than climbed.

Leo leaned in close, until April felt his breath. She shrugged her shoulder at the chills it gave her.

"Do you know where my cock is, April Nightingale?"

"No," she breathed.

"It is almost right against you. I'm so close to being inside you. Can you feel it April Nightingale?"

"You must stop saying my name like that."

"Why must I?"

"Because you will unravel me."

"That is my purpose. *April. Nightingale.*"

Leo's breath washed over her lips, and she waited to be kissed. Instead she felt the warm tip of his cock tap against her entrance, leaving a silky bead of cum to mingle with her own moisture.

Her body arched in response.

"Do you remember when I washed you here?"

His hand came up between them, and she shivered as his finger tucked under her neckline to trace the upper curves of her breasts.

She nodded.

"I cannot hear you, love."

"I do," she breathed.

Hearing her name on his lips had been one thing —as lovely as her silly name had ever sounded—but the casual moniker of "love" made her heart stand still. Was it a word she would ever again be possessed in the name of?

"And when I washed you here?" His hand whisked around back of her, sliding past her raised hem to the top of her ass.

"Yes."

He slid lower, till his fingers curled between her legs from behind, dipping over the scrunched fabric of her skirts. His finger circled the rim of her entrance.

His cheek pushed sidelong against hers and hot, bullish breath washed over her ear, "And here?"

He did not wait for her to answer but responded to her raised, seeking hips by splaying her with his fingers and thrusting into her with one filling, fluid stroke.

April had held her breath for that moment, for that sensation, for the revisiting of their carnal pleasures. Yet his penetration added little to the effusion of thrills coursing through her. She already had what she had longed for just by being in his arms. Just by sharing space in the dark.

She bracketed her legs against the walls of the narrow steps and stifled a moan against her lover's lips. He pulled away and thrust again, withdrawing slowly to spread her slick warmth and guide him better.

Her lips pinched against her own teeth as he kissed her hard and thrust again. He increased his pace.

The stairs cut into her back, but it didn't matter. Leo was a specter devoted to their mutual pleasure. Everything else just sort of... disappeared.

His hungry thrusts pierced deep, chasing her upward a step or two. And he followed like a hunter, finding her slick cusp again even when he slipped out in his vigor.

At one such point, she seized the chance to change positions. He left a hand on her, feeling what she was doing. His hand slid to her ass as she flipped over, kneeling on the steps above him.

She knew he could find her in the dark. Was

certain he would at any moment and she waited for him to take her by the hips and draw himself into her from behind.

But he didn't.

Instead, his chin nestled between her thighs, coming up from under her. And his tongue laved her from stem to stern with thrilling new access.

April bit off the unconscionable sound that rose within her, squeaking instead. A gentle laugh vibrated against her mound.

Leo parted her and tongued her quim with the same voracity as his kisses above the neck.

She had never, *never*, been drunk of so adoringly. She fought the urge to unclench herself. To let that burst happen too soon within her. The longer she held onto it, the more... *the more...*

"Let it go," he whispered, nuzzling between her cheeks.

She imagined what they would look like in broad daylight. How salacious, how ridiculous. A little smile of pride warmed her lips as she realized to what soaring heights she had sown her wild oats.

It was the sort of scandal that would take *one hundred* marriages to smooth over, should they be caught. And he had offered her at least one. He had said he would wed her...

Leo indulged in another languid lick that fell against her like a word of reassurance. She floated up and away, becoming distant, not from the act of her devouring, but from the way she had tightened against it. And then...

She came.

She came so hard she *screamed*.

12

Leo did not linger between April's spasming thighs. Had she just *screamed?*

He imagined the whole crowd of April's sedate cousins becoming a mob with pitchforks. At the helm would surely be her mother, perhaps shouting, *"Off with his head!"*

He winced, cursing his imagination.

But there was no time to linger on omens and nightmares, and he was already shoving April forward and up with a hand on her right ass cheek.

They lurched up the steps, clumsily striking every unseen bit of wood paneling, as they tried to right themselves and escape. Stealth was dispensed with. Flight was the more pertinent thing.

They came to a small landing just as Leo

succeeded at getting two buttons of his fall refastened. He reached for what he'd identified as a door by the slash of dull light coming from its base. But at the jiggle of his hand on the knob, April swatted him away.

"No. We must keep going up. To the attic." She took his hand and put it on the rail of a much steeper, almost ladder-like, set of steps.

Confused murmurs collected at the foot of the staircase and someone gave the jammed door a feeble try.

Leo and April ascended to the garret, panting. He turned around as soon as April had closed the hatch in the floor.

"Why did you scream?!" he hissed.

"Why did *you* run?"

He whipped his head, trying to shake off his confusion. "Why did I—? I *ran* because you screamed. Because those gathered for your *engagement* tea heard you scream."

Somehow, she looked as confused as he, even after his perfectly lucid explanation.

"Because you said you would wed me. So I... I thought—"

"You thought that the best way to go about it? To humiliate ourselves? To show your family our backsides?"

"No!" She protested. "In the throes of your intimate attentions, I did not exactly think things through."

Leo swooped toward her, wanting to shake some sense into her by her pretty shoulders—shoulders which she shrugged, disarming him immediately.

"I think a part of me also just wanted to run with you. To sneak off. As we did before."

Now there was a wish he could understand. She smiled, and he could not help but smile with her against the dread of those gathering belowstairs. Her reasoning, so absurd on its surface, was perfectly intertwined with his own.

He reached up and played with a lock of hair that had fallen to her shoulder. "We had already snuck off."

"I wished to sneak further. To pull you deeper into my house. Into this rabbit's hole. Into my life."

There was something in her words he'd not seen before. Something hidden. Something tucked deep between her brazen encouragements. Something vulnerable and insecure.

"Did you not believe me when I said I would wed you?"

She stood still for a long time, and the silence in the attic made the distant chatter at the foot of the stairs more evident.

Her blue eyes looked up at him. "I am engaged to Mr. Gramble because I have been told he is a miracle. A miracle in that he would have me. In that he has spent much time in the Americas and is not embedded in the local web of gossip."

"And what does the local web of gossip have to say about you?"

"That I take my errands alone too often. That I come home too disheveled. That I—" she looked to the floorboards and up again, interrupted by a distant bang on the stairwell door. "That I disappear at gatherings for long stretches." She smiled, wistful and distant before continuing. "What would the talented son of wealthy lineage want here? With me? With all that salaciousness swirling about?"

"I think you know how I feel about the salacious part."

"But I don't. Because it was never that way in any tryst or dalliance I've ever had. I was enjoyed by the others in one way and one way only. It is so ingrained in me as an expectation, that I could not fathom otherwise. And then here you are. Not a miracle to my family, but a miracle to me. So miraculous I struggle to accept it. What is there about me that could recommend me for marriage? For marriage..."

Leo stepped toward her until her back was against the lone garret window.

"...for marriage to one such as you?"

Leo cupped her cheek in his hand. Her skin was so soft. He stroked his thumb across her lips and over the little mole above her lip. He waited until her lips fell slightly ajar.

"April, I did not return home from my travels knowing anything that I wanted in life. But then I fell through the little gap in someone's smile. I held hands with a stranger and entered her realm of swan theft and sneaking about. In her world I am younger. In her world, I trust that everything will turn out all right. That there will be a light beyond every darkness as time marches on. In her world, swans are not merely birds but are wings on which she rests her hopes, and she has taught me to hope as she does. To trust in hope even when it threatens to end me."

A tear slid down the side of Leo's finger where he cradled her cheek. Her lips peeled into that smile— the one that gave him chills and sent him falling all over again into a little gap.

"I was reminded, recently, of the first map I ever drew. It was a treasure map. And do you know where the treasure lay, my love?"

She shook her head, speechless as she reached up to place her hand over his.

"X marked the spot just over the berm. I do not remember if I knew you then. But somehow, I knew there was treasure here. You are that treasure."

April wiped her eyes and shied away from him, turning toward the window.

She looked out as she tamed gentle sobs. Leo waited, patient.

"I see two white spots out there," she said. "On Derring pond. I wish I could have seen it. Seen them together."

Leo considered whether or not to tell her just how distressing some of the bird rutting had been, but she turned back around before he could decide.

"I threw Gerald over the berm late last night. I could not sleep thinking about today. And you are right. I am full of hopes and wishes. And he was the vessel of my wish as I saw him back to his favorite pond. To his happiness."

Leo's smile could have eclipsed the sun then, as April Nightingale stood there, crying happy tears in an attic with him.

"It worked," she said. "My wish came true."

Leo wrapped her in his arms just as she began to shudder with sobs.

A great *bang* came from downstairs as the door to the stairwell was breached.

Leo drew back just enough to see her. "April Nightingale, we are about to be caught."

She nodded, laughing softly through the tears.

"So will you marry me?" he whispered. "Will you put on the most compromising of displays with me?"

"Yes, Mr. Derring. Yes, I will."

She kissed him then, pulling his face down to hers with both hands. Her knee skimmed up the side of his leg and he obligingly held it against his hip.

They kissed through the flurry of footsteps on the hollow stairs. They kissed through concerned calls of April's name. They kissed through confused murmurs at the foot of the ladder. They kissed through another loud *bang*.

And then they kissed in silence, falling genuinely back into their lovers' ways before realizing something was amiss.

It was *too* silent.

13

April lowered her leg, strangely disappointed that the hounds had been called off.

"Where did they all go?" asked Leo.

April frowned. "I wish I knew." She lifted her skirt and padded quickly to the closed hatch. She knelt and put an ear to the boards.

She looked back at Leo, who mouthed: *Nothing?* She shook her head at him, charmed by his bewildered expression.

But then there was something. Muted shouting from the upstairs halls. She could not make it out.

Leo hissed in warning as she opened the hatch. But no one was in the stairwell. Instead, the voices came from the upstairs door that adjoined the landing. They grew louder, clearer. She heard Agatha's name and was propelled down the steep attic steps by a flare of interest. Leo soon stepped down onto the landing beside her.

Voices were clear now on the other side of the door: "Oh! How could you?!" April's mother spat the words between bursts of relentless, inconsolable weeping.

April's brow pinched in confusion as she held an ear to the door.

Leo leaned close to her. "Shall we reveal ourselves?" he whispered.

April was unsure. She put a finger up between them, asking that he wait. She carefully opened the door to the upstairs hall and peered past it, finding the backs of a small crowd gathered at the corridor's end. No one seemed to notice her, focused as they were on whatever was happening.

Certain of the group's distraction, April wandered out. Leaving the door ajar was all it took to coax Leo to follow her. She felt him at her back as she began to nudge through the gathering toward her mother's cries. They came from the neglected guest room at the hall's end.

April swam through a little sea of onlookers. They parted for her, but watched her with eerie interest, seemingly awaiting her reaction to whatever lay ahead. She arrived at the edge of the crowd in the middle of the bedchamber and finally saw what the others strained to see: a glimpse of Agatha sitting on the edge of the bed, hanging her head. And Mr. Gramble, April's betrothed, pacing nervously in his shirtsleeves.

April did not quite comprehend at first, until Agatha lifted her eyes and a smirk cut through her look of shame. Agatha and Mr. Gramble had been in the room together, *alone*. And unlike all the years of suspicion swirling around April, *they* had really and truly been caught.

April's jaw went slack in astonishment, yet she could not help a twitch in her cheek. She covered her lips—her *smile*—with her hands as she approached. "Oh, dear sister, what have you done?"

It was then she realized that Leo was at her side. She looked up, finding his expression to be equally agape, if not yet fully comprehending.

April was caught by surprise as her mother dove into her arms for comfort.

"Your sister has compromised herself."

"It will be all right, Mama." April petted her mother's heaving back.

Mr. Gramble surged toward them. "I can explain."

But April shook her head at him. She'd not squander such a beautifully public opportunity to sever their engagement.

"Oh, Mr. Gramble," she said gravely, still comforting her mother. "I thought I was to wed an honorable man, but—" she shrugged. "I would sooner wed a stranger than yourself."

"But the banns have been read."

"And they say *Miss Nightingale*, do they not? You may wed *that* Miss Nightingale instead." April pointed at her sister on the bed.

Then April looked around at those gathered. Each pretended to look at the floor, as though they were innocent of eavesdropping. "With so many witnesses, I dare say you have no choice."

Mr. Gramble raked long fingers through his silver hair and thrust out his jaw. But he said nothing. Merely turned away to pace again.

April's mother looked up at her and sniffled. "Where have you been? We were looking all over." She noticed Leo, and her red eyes squinted in suspicion. "And you..."

Leo and April shared an instinctive shrug and smiled.

"We were discussing the mating rituals of swans," said April.

"And I had one of the peaches," added Leo. "It was delicious."

April caught the flinch of a narrowly-resisted wink in her lover.

"We heard the commotion upstairs, the same as everyone, and came to see," said April. "It is a pity. I dare say things are ruined now." *Gloriously, perfectly ruined*, she thought. *Just as herself.*

Sensing her mother's discomfort was the most real in the room, she helped her to straighten up. "It will be all right, Mama. Trust that it will."

Some of those gathered lost interest in the scene —or deemed it too scandalous to further associate with—and removed themselves.

April approached Agatha and took her hand, urging her to get up and follow her to the far corner of the room. She had to be sure of one thing. April lowered her voice to a whisper. "I must know that you chose this... that Mr. Gramble did not force anything on—"

"Of course I did," spat Agatha. "And I enjoyed every second of it."

April was not shocked that her sister had done what she thought to be a hurtful thing to her. Nor was she shocked Agatha had been caught. Agatha did not have the years of subterfuge behind her to succeed at such a tryst—to not have it bubble up as any more than rumors. Agatha always glided through existence with the confidence that nothing could touch her.

"Who found you?" asked April.

Agatha did not answer but crossed her arms and nodded in the direction of the departing onlookers. Anna was revealed standing there as others left the room around her. She tucked her lips between her teeth, trying to contain a smile.

April smiled back at Anna and patted Agatha on the shoulder. "Do not be so bleak, sister. You will get what you wish. Mr. Gramble's wealth and protection. Only look! You have industriously secured it for yourself." April dusted her hands. "I am free of it."

Her eyes met Leo's. He was incapable of hiding his delight. His smile was broad. His dimple, deep. And April would trip and fall into that dimple, just as he had fallen into the gap between her teeth.

Like Gerald, she had fallen in love with the wrong swan, and she was ready for whatever dance was required to tie herself to this cob forever.

14

Leo enjoyed the view as April slid her bare arms up and down along the blanket as though she could fly. The sun came out from behind the clouds, bathing her breasts in golden light. The dew from the cool grass could be felt through the blanket beneath his bare knees.

He bent to trail kisses down her neck before dismounting from his position and urging her to roll onto her side. Then he took a place beside her and pulled her back against him until they were sealed together.

She rubbed her head against his chin as he entered her, and she whispered between gentle moans: "I am yours. I am yours."

And she was. She was his. And they were celebrating their marriage beside the pond where he had found her. Where she had emerged from the muck like the Lady of the Lake—or some comical version thereof.

They had agreed, for the sake of their families, to engage in a formal, *chaste* courtship—besides, of course, the moment they stole in the hackney on the way back from town, or the time Leo left the coffee house five minutes before her and met her in an alley. *Besides* those times, they had been flawlessly chaste. And it had nearly ended him to keep his hands off her.

Because all the teas with the Nightingales and all the strolls on the berm had fed his perpetual study of her but had not changed that which he knew from the start. That she was a rare bird. That there were no others who would take him by the hand and be so ridiculous with him... So brazen. So sensual.

There were many things he'd not yet known when he asked her to wed him. Like that she wished for a Havanese puppy or that she could not do simple maths without her fingers, yet could estimate the acreage of a property with stunning accuracy. And when she had said she gardened, she meant that she could propagate virtually anything from a cutting. The only thing he'd known—that they had *both* known—was their tendency toward play. Their shared appreciation of holding onto glimmers of youth. A trait that would fill Derring Hall with laughter should they one day be blessed with children of their own—something else he learned they both hoped for.

"You are thinking very hard right now, I can tell."

"Only of you," he tried. But it was no use, she knew him too well.

"Do not think of me," she pleaded. "Only feel me, right now. Be with me."

She pushed her hips back against him to strengthen her point, and his mind went white like he'd stolen a glimpse at the sun. There was no reason for hesitation or fear now.

She strained to look past her shoulder at him, and he basked in the glow of her gap-toothed smile. Her body tightened against him as they groaned in unison. His cock throbbed inside her. His breath quickened, as did his pace...

They braced themselves against one another, against the impending corruption of their senses. When he finally came inside her, it was a shot of bliss, his final strokes being eased by the presence of his seed. She shuddered, pressing her back so ardently against him that he thought they would never come undone from one another. *So be it.*

Halting exhales racked their bodies and rendered them a heaving pile of limp appendages.

Leo drew a deep breath and let himself slide from her warm body—after all, he could forever return. There were no farewells now. He rolled her over and tucked his face against her chest. Her skin was dewy and she smelled like something sweet.

She raised a hand to the back of his head. His hair went more curly whenever he sweat, and she pushed it back behind his ears. He peeked under her arm toward the pond. Two swans, perfectly framed.

He and April had started calling the king's swan Rosemary .

April noticed him looking at her and shifted herself to sit. "I wish I had seen their courtship ritual."

"You will have many seasons more to see it."

She shrugged and stroked his hair again before he shimmied to sit up beside her.

"Was it as extravagant as ours?"

Leo laughed. April's wedding frock lay crumpled not a few feet away. "Not nearly so, and they did not have to have the banns read three weeks before."

April threw up her arms. "But if they *had* made an announcement, I would not be living in the regret of not seeing it!"

Leo kissed her shoulder and pulled her against him. "I vow I will never let you miss the sight of a rutting birds for the rest of our days."

"Why did you not include that in your vows at the church?"

"Because your mother was in the front pew."

April laughed.

It was true though. He would never let her miss a thing. He would go to her as he had that fateful day of the tea to tell her any little thing that might bring her joy. Which reminded him... he had to show her the clutch of eggs he had spotted in the reeds.

In turn, he knew she would keep life—and Derring Hall—full and bright. But Derring Hall was not yet empty...

Epilogue

Mrs. Nightingale lifted her skirts with one hand and tightened her grip on the basket with her other. Careful of her hem, she made her way up the berm, practicing apologies in her head. She just had to make it to the door. Just had to bang the knocker and beg the butler to let her see the elder Derring. She would politely leave the basket if refused.

But her plans were undone by the time she reached the top of the berm. Because she was greeted with a sight she had not seen for years: Isambard Derring in his rose garden.

He'd not yet noticed her.

"Mr. Derring?"

He looked up and she was pleasantly surprised to find him smiling. He put a hand on his knee and picked up the cane from the mulch beside him. She longed to rush down the hill, to help him stand but was still unsure of her welcome.

Thankfully, he got up quite well, if with visible effort. Her shoulders relaxed.

"Mrs. Nightingale," he called. "How good to see you." His eyes darted between her and the half-pruned bushes around him.

"Is it?" she asked, knowing the question to be forward, perhaps more impertinent than she had ever dared be, but she had to know. Perhaps a bit of April had gotten into her.

Mr. Derring's smile strengthened and he waved her the rest of the way down the hill to join him.

She'd not seen him for so long. His hair was longer, wispier, whiter... but he still had broad, solid shoulders even if his coat sleeves fit more loosely. He still had tenderness in his brown eyes when he looked at his roses... and at her.

A stray hank of gray-blonde hair fell into Mrs. Nightingale's eyes. She bent forward to meet her thumb and shove the hair back under her mob cap, realizing, belatedly, that she'd lifted her hem rather high in doing so.

Derring did not seem to notice. He held out a hand when she was near and removed the burden of her basket.

"For you," she said, already panting from her short jaunt.

His eyes went wide, smoothing out his crows' feet. "What have I done to deserve your kindness?"

Mrs. Nightingale dropped her hem and folded her hands. "You have weathered my unexplained ire for a decade. I do not even know whether you are aware of it. But I am both aware and regretful. Please, forgive me."

Mr. Derring looked at the covered basket before bending slowly to set it on the grass. "And here I thought you were here because our families had been brought together by a marriage."

She looked away, sensitive to whether she was being teased. "That too."

"Will you walk with me, Mrs. Nightingale?"

A little rush went through her as his arm was proffered. She took it, and he turned them down the length of his rose garden's path. It extended all the way down the east side of the manor, crunched into the narrow corridor between Derring Hall and the berm.

She felt him lean more on her than his cane and she straightened, feeling regal beside him. They both stood taller together. The silence of walking with him was beautiful, yet anxiety forced her to speak. "It has been a long time since I have seen you out here. For a time, I thought you dead—I mean... I worried you dead. Imagine my relief when I saw you at the wedding."

The elder Derring laughed. The sound was warm and light, an invitation to laugh with him. She cracked a smile.

"Yes. I've not come outside as much as I ought. Leo has often chided me for it. And it is true also that I've ailed from time to time. I regret that I could not linger after the nuptials, but I was still getting my strength back."

Mrs. Nightingale squeezed his arm, hoping to convey a concern she didn't know how to express with words. "It is not easy, these years of our lives."

"Easy, no. But not without blessings."

He stopped their walk beside a small bird bath in the path's center and pointed behind him to the house. "Do you know what finally got me out of the house, Mrs. Nightingale?"

"I do not."

"My son, of course, always tried to get me out for air. And a part of me wanted desperately to listen to him, because he was right. But I did not start coming out merely because of his badgering."

"Then why did you?"

"Because he married your daughter. Because I could not go to a wedding in my banyan and slippers. I had to go outside and be a person. And for all my creaks and complaints, I enjoyed it. And now I am oft chased outside by the raucousness of those lovebirds."

Mrs. Nightingale's hand went to her lips as she looked up at the windows above. It was for the best that Derring did not elaborate.

He put a hand on hers where it rested in his arm, and she was glad she had not put on gloves.

"The young have a way of helping us circle back sometimes to our own youths. We can resent which parts of it we can no longer grasp, or we can seize which parts of it we can."

His thumb stroked the back of Mrs. Nightingale's hand. Her chest heaved tight behind her stays.

"You are granted a slap across my face if my next question is too bold or my assumption, too wrong-headed..."

"What is your question?" Her heart faltered as his eyes met hers. The brown in them was faded, but the spark in them, eternal.

"I thought you might have carried a torch for me back then."

A nervous breath burst from her, and she squirmed under his gaze.

He dropped his cane and put a gentle hand on her shoulder, steadying her.

"Mr. Derring, I—"

"I do not ask to embarrass you. I would never."

She didn't know whether it was his hand on her

shoulder or his gentle eyes, but she found the courage to look squarely back up at him.

"I did," she said. "I did. I love my gardens and I was lonely. When I saw you tending your roses each day, it lit a spark of hope in me for companionship. I never meant to linger or bother you or—"

"You needn't make your case for it. I understand completely. I was lonesome too, Mrs. Nightingale." He took her hands in his. "Only, this garden did not start as mine, but as my wife's. The loss of her was very fresh when I first saw you on the hill, and I had to be alone. So I must apologize too, for creating some misunderstanding of disinterest."

Mrs. Nightingale had fretted the taking of her hands... had felt an apology coming and did not know if it would be one of rejection. But no, he had called it a *misunderstanding of disinterest.* She reached cautiously for the hope in that, realizing she had come for reasons beyond neighborly reconciliation. Though, she swore to herself, she could live with that outcome too.

She looked down at her hands in his and instinctively looked over her shoulder toward home, as though a mother of her own still resided there and would scold her. As though she, an elder widow, was compromising herself. She surprised herself by smiling at the thought.

"You are right, Mr. Derring. There are parts of youth yet to be seized."

"Please, call me Isambard. We must get to know one another better."

He gave her his arm again and they continued to stroll.

"I am sorry," she said. "I should have thought of how near it was to Mrs. Derring's passing. Before... before eating fruit at you like a moonstruck adolescent."

Isambard laughed. "I am glad we are in conversation again, Mrs. Nightingale. Thanks to the wild ways of our progeny."

Yet again, Mrs. Nightingale found herself wishing not to know details on how wild.

As though on cue, a loud crash and peals of laughter came from an open upstairs window above them.

Mrs. Nightingale smiled up at it. Her daughter was happy.

"April brings a lot of laughter to Derring Hall. She will keep it filled with life," said Isambard.

It was Mrs. Nightingale who stopped them then and looked into the man's glittering eyes. "Just remember," she said, "that Derring Hall is not yet empty."

Dear Reader,

Thanks for joining me for this little adventure. If you'd like to stay in touch about future releases and freebies, consider signing up for my news-letter, Daria's Dossier, at my website:

www.dariavernon.com

or follow me on social:

instagram.com/daria.vernon.romance

tiktok.com/@authordariav

twitter.com/authordariav